ECHOES OF MY HOMELAND

Óscar Ribas

Translated with an Introduction by Clive Willis

FAOILEÁN/SEAGULL

NUI MAYNOOTH
Ollscoil na hÉireann Má Nuad

University of
BRISTOL

Author: Óscar Ribas
Original Title: *Ecos da Minha Terra*, Luanda, Lello, 1952.
Translator: Clive Willis
Cover: Stefan Edelbroek
Publisher: Faoileán/Seagull
Orders: HiPLA
   School of Modern Languages
   15 Woodland Road
   University of Bristol
   Bristol BS8 1TE
   England
http://www.bristol.ac.uk/hispanic/
© 2006 by Faoileán/Seagull and Clive Willis
ISBN 0-9553922-3-3
   978-0-9553922-3-8

Table of Contents

INTRODUCTION

Óscar Ribas has made four significant contributions to Angolan fiction, all of them composed after he gradually lost his eyesight from congenital retinitis. The malady began when he was in his twenties and completed its baleful course when he was thirty-six years old. The four works are the 'novels' *Uanga* ('Magic Spells', 1951) and *Tudo Isto Aconteceu* ('All This Happened', 1975) and the collections of short stories to be found in *Ecos da Minha Terra* ('Echoes of My Homeland', 1952) and in *Quilanduquilo* ('Time to Relax', 1973). In the case of *Uanga*, the term 'novel' is used hesitantly, owing to the fact that the work is heavily documentary in its impact. Indeed, it was none other than Captain Henrique Galvão, a man with strong Angolan connections and later celebrated, in 1961, for leading the anti-Salazar hi-jacking of the Portuguese cruise ship, the *Santa Maria*, who was the first to describe the work as a 'fictionalized documentary'. Ribas himself applied the designation 'fictionalized autobiography' to *Tudo Isto Aconteceu.*

Óscar Bento Ribas was born in the Angolan capital, Luanda, in 1909, the eldest son of a white Portuguese immigrant civil servant and a black Angolan washerwoman. He received good secondary education in Luanda, where he lived with his parents and two brothers. With his father, he travelled three times to Portugal in his teens and early twenties. His father's professional relocations meant that the family regularly moved on, so that Ribas also became well acquainted with

Angola's second city, Benguela, and with townships and villages between those two centres, not solely on the coast but also in the interior. In those settings he acquired a profound and virtually unequalled anthropological and cultural knowledge of the two major ethnic groups of those areas, the Kimbundu (around Luanda) and (further south, around Benguela) the Ovimbundu (Umbundu in the singular). In 1937, on their father's death, Ribas settled with his two brothers in Luanda. Owing to his failing eyesight he was unable to find regular employment (other than some intermittent primary-school teaching) but was greatly supported by his two brothers in the transcription of his early jottings and later in the setting down of his dictation. Later he mastered Braille and established in 1972, in Luanda, the Instituto Óscar Ribas for the education of the blind. In the light of his visual difficulties one can only marvel at his extensive output, derived from painstaking acquisition of material from a rich variety of sources.

In his late teens Ribas had already published two novellas in very limited editions, but his first mature work (apart from occasional newspaper articles) did not appear until 1948. Published in Luanda (as were nearly all his works) and entitled *Flores e Espinhos* ('Flowers and Thorns'), it was a collection of poems, essays and short tales that made no great impact, though it later enjoyed the curious distinction of being reprinted in Liechtenstein. Much more successful was *Uanga*. This work met with no little acclaim, not only in Angola, but also from critics in Lisbon, Rio de Janeiro and São Paulo. In Lisbon the Agência-Geral do Ultramar (the General Overseas Agency) awarded it an 'honourable mention'. A translation into German was undertaken by an Austrian scholar, Dr Alfred Radspieler, but apparently remains unpublished. The warm reception accorded to *Uanga* by critics in Portugal, Brazil and

Angola was to be redoubled when the revised and augmented edition appeared in 1969. Sundry later editions were to follow.

Recognition outside the Portuguese-speaking world was, however, to be focussed, in 1952, on the short story 'A Praga' ('The Curse'). Casually submitted by Ribas to the International Committee on Christian Literature, which was based in London, it was awarded the Margaret Wrong Memorial Prize, attributed in 1952 to entries forwarded from sub-Saharan Africa. Subsequently it appeared, in Peter Sulzer's German translation, in two anthologies published in Switzerland. 'A Praga' was to become one of the ten stories contained in *Ecos da Minha Terra*, of which the present volume is the first English translation. Prior to the present text, the only other published English version of Ribas's work was a partial rendering of the short story 'A Medalha' ('The Medal') which appeared in W. H. Whiteley's *A Selection of African Prose* (UNESCO, 1965). This elegant tale was to become one of the components of the collection entitled *Quilanduquilo*.

Uanga is set in the Luanda of 1882. It is a tale of spite and retaliation, as an illiterate black man misinterprets a letter and creates havoc in a marriage. Much emphasis is placed on the roles of medicine men and vengeful witchdoctors, as well as on prayers to Saint Anthony, but in the end none of these measures takes effect. Yet the narrative is often secondary to an anthropological display. *Uanga* is rich in folklore: in particular, spells and recipes, songs and dances are all expressed in detail. The frequent songs are presented in Portuguese translation, but the Kimbundu originals feature in an appendix. The world of the *kimbandas* (medicine men) and of the baleful *feiticeiros* (witchdoctors or sorcerers) is closely explored and implicitly condemned as both ineffectual and rooted in the greed of its practitioners. At times the text is supported by extensive explanatory footnotes. Moreover, there is provided a lengthy glossary, in order to translate and explain the full meaning of the many African words that appear in the body of the text. Frequently, the original Kimbundu words (and, elsewhere, in other later texts, words in Umbundu) are shown to have undergone considerable metamorphosis in their passage into Angolan Portuguese, thus presenting a triple strand (original word, Angolan Portuguese and standard Portuguese translation). In both these respects, folklore and language, Ribas was establishing a pattern that was to prevail, in varying degree, in all his subsequent works. He eventually published, in 1997, a major dictionary of Angolan regionalisms, much of its contents being assembled from the sundry glossaries to his other works.

After *Ecos da Minha Terra* (to which we shall return) Ribas began to send abroad, and especially to Brazil, large numbers of copies of both that work and *Uanga*. The outcome was that between 1954 and 1957 he received honorary membership of five institutes in Brazil and one in Argentina, all of them learned bodies concerned with folklore and comparative cultural issues. With the incentive of the strong ethnic ties of Angola with much of the black population of Brazil, Ribas now threw himself into the production of a series of studies devoted to Angolan folklore. *Ilundo* ('Religion', 1959) was devoted to a detailed analysis of Angolan animism and its rituals, while the three volumes of *Missosso* ('Traditions', 1961-64) provided a treasure-house of brief traditional folktales, fables, songs, prayers, incantations, proverbs, recipes and conundrums. Further honours followed in Angola, Portugal and Brazil, in conjunction with several invited visits to both of the latter countries, which, in turn, involved contacts with major scholars. In 1964, in Salvador, in Brazil, the University of Bahia published his *Usos e Costumes Angolanos*, an essay on Angolan customs. Other works that followed were *Alimentação Regional Angolana* ('Angolan Regional Cookery', 1965 and sundry later editions), *Izomba* ('Recreation', 1965), and *Sunguilando* ('Folktales at Sunset', 1967). A book of verse,

Cultuando as Musas ('In Cult to the Muses') appeared in 1993 and a collection of essays, proverbs and further 'snapshots' was published in 2002 under the title *Temas da Vida Angolana e Suas Incidências.* Its author was aged ninety-three.

Ribas has accomplished vital, outstanding and, as yet, unsurpassed work in the preservation of Angola's cultural patrimony. His work in ethnographical and anthropological studies in respect of the Kimbundu and Ovimbundu amplified the pioneering studies on the Kimbundu people of Héli Châtelain at the end of the nineteenth century and complements the researches of Ribas's own contemporary, Carlos Estermann, on the peoples of south-west and central Angola. In *Tudo Isto Aconteceu* (p. 475) he wrote as follows: 'My work embodies two major concerns: one is to build up a record of oral literature before it should fall into total oblivion or suffer the contempt of the 'civilized' world; the other is to proclaim the truth about the black man's ability, which has been so sadly dismissed for so long. My aim is to demonstrate to the Angolans of the future the intellectual output of their forebears, as well as to restore the black man to his proper place by revealing the man that he is, and not the ape that he has been claimed to be.'

His place as an anthropologist was assured, but in 1973 he returned, in part, to generating his own creative fiction with the publication of *Quilanduquilo.* In primary position in this collection are nine of Ribas's own short stories, though they are followed by four brief traditional tales and fifty-eight 'snapshots' or snippets of anthropological interest, much characterized by lively human situations and ample use of dialogue. These 'snapshots' provide a valuable and vibrant record of day-to-day life in Ribas's Angola. As for his own nine short stories, they cover a variety of themes: the white immigrant's varied success in search of his fortune, the social problems of those of mixed race, nineteenth-century slavery, polygamy, racial intermarriage, curses and spells, and, in the characters' muddled syncretism, as illustrated in 'A Medalha', traditional beliefs in the powers of ancient spirits at odds with Christian appeals to Saint Anthony. In his Introduction Ribas asserts that all these stories were based on real-life episodes.

The autobiographical 'novel' *Tudo Isto Aconteceu* was written between 1962 and late in 1974. Its closing chapter was composed after the fall of Portugal's authoritarian regime in April of that latter year. At last, Ribas could find more open expression for ideas that would have been unwelcome to the regimes of António Salazar and Marcello Caetano. The protagonist of this lengthy 'novel' is named Osvaldo Relvas, while the narrative is set down in the third person, beginning in 1904 with the arrival in Luanda of the Portuguese immigrant Armando Relvas, Osvaldo's father. The thinly disguised pseudonym becomes almost pointless once the reader begins to recognize that the progressively sightless Osvaldo is the author of works bearing the same titles as those of Ribas himself. The Brazilian honours are also identical to those received by Ribas, and there is clearly an end to all pretence when 'Osvaldo' meets named non-fictional Portuguese and Brazilian men of letters, most notably the distinguished Brazilian folklorist Luís da Câmara Cascudo, with whom he formed a mutually valued academic relationship.

The closing chapter heralds the approach of Angolan independence in the wake of the overthrow of Portugal's 'despotic regime', which had cramped that country and her colonies for almost half a century. The independence struggle had begun in 1961 on the very day after Henrique Galvão had surrendered the *Santa Maria* to the Brazilian authorities in Recife, when once he had been forced to abandon his related project to sail to the coast of Angola to add his promotional skills to the planned uprising. Ribas reveals how 1974 had brought bitter and shameful violence to the streets of Luanda, promoted in particular by hotheads among the white population. He examines the attitudes of the extremists on both sides and nervously steers a middle course, pointing to the benefits that the Europeans had brought to Angola as well as to the recent outrages committed by whites and blacks alike.

But Ribas's position as a tolerant, even-handed and generous man of mixed blood could never fully align itself with the Marxist regime that eventually came to power after the struggles of 1975 and 1976. Most of the white population rapidly dispersed. It was hardly surprising that the new and independent Angola was one in which he would become temporarily marginalized as a figure purportedly once favoured by European imperialism and, indeed, by 'Fascist' authoritarianism. In 1983 Ribas left a still convulsive Angola and settled in Cascais in a newly democratic Portugal, in order to spend his remaining years there, at the Santa Casa da Misericórdia, and there to obtain medical treatment for his blind wife Cândida. His house in Luanda was to be taken over by the Angolan government and converted into a museum. Rather belatedly, his native land recognized his true worth more fully when, in 1989, he was awarded the Diploma of Merit by the Ministry of Culture.

The present volume, *Echoes of My Homeland (Ecos da Minha Terra)*, is arguably the most assured of Ribas's ventures into fiction. Here there is no genre difficulty, unlike the instances of the two 'novels', nor is it a mixed batch, unlike the case of the tripartite *Quilanduquilo*. However, some of the ten short stories are obviously of Ribas's own devising (for example, 'People of the Sea' or 'Night of Nostalgia'), while others (like 'Damba Maria' or 'Bango-a-Mussungo' or 'Hebo') are evidently extended versions of erstwhile folktales. The collection is subtitled *Dramas Angolanos*: the ten stories seek to exhibit dramatic situations, past and present, in the everyday life and folklore of Angola. It was Ribas's modest view that his stories made a contribution to what he described as the 'great ethnographic monument' of his country, and in this he was a major precursor of the more recent quest for *angolanidade* ('Angolan cultural values').

Ribas's qualities as a writer (equalled by few of his compatriots) stem from four main starting-points, all of which are present in *Echoes*: closely documented knowledge of his subject-matter, a moving and genuine lyricism, psychological depth and intellectual honesty. His writing is not overtly politically motivated; it neither attacks colonialism, nor does it have anything good to say in its favour, for such considerations are not Ribas's concern. Rather, his interest lies in the situation of the individual, his or her joys, fears, loves, ambitions; it is this aspect that will probably give his work a more lasting value than that of much of the more pamphleteering and revolutionary Angolan literature that inevitably (and not unjustifiably) dominated the last quarter of the twentieth century.

He does have things to condemn: the internal slave-trade (operated by black or by white), exploitation (by black or by white), tyranny (by black or by white); he censures greed and hatred. As a *mestiço* (a person of mixed blood), he is in a position from which it soon becomes clear that he is able to 'probe the skull' of both blacks and whites alike and that, with one exception, he does so without artificiality. Both races are portrayed with sympathy, but with all their defects plainly visible. Ribas can write with the same depth of feeling about the reactions of an illiterate white peasant immigrant (as in 'The Poor and Meek') as he can of a black girl sold by her uncle into slavery (as in 'Damba Maria'). He can interpret the psyche of those haunted by centuries-old superstition (as in 'The Curse'), though we are left perplexed as to how this tale could win a prize for Christian literature. However, one story, 'Night of Nostalgia', strikes an arguably jarring and unsuccessful note, in that it caricatures or parodies (intentionally or otherwise) the white settler's sentimentality. It relates a Christmas dinner-party on a remote farmstead.

The three major participants (the farmer, a trader and a district officer) are whites who all express a cloying homesickness for Portugal; they also drink an enthusiastic toast to the land that they have now adopted, eagerly prompted by the mixed-race wife of the farmer. This story constitutes the one weakness in an otherwise fascinating collection.

Of the ten stories, one ('Hebo') is a popular legend, a sort of magical *Taming of the Shrew*; another ('Which Hurts More?') is a timeless narrative set in ethnic custom and is based on a trial of courage. A third story ('Bango-a-Mussungo') dates probably from the thirteenth or fourteenth century and is derived from a legend concerning a tyrant's fate, arising from his decision to be buried alive in a vain attempt to become immortal. Of the remainder, two are taken from the end of the eighteenth century, and five are enacted at some point in the first half of the twentieth century. Six of the stories (including the three mentioned at the beginning of this paragraph) are concerned exclusively with black people (though in two of them the existence of white colonialism is alluded to). Three of the tales focus on the effects of that colonialism and on the juxtaposition of the two cultures.

Magic and witchcraft find a role in several of the tales, while some of the stories, most notably 'The Thief and the Sorcerer' and 'People of the Sea', have shorter legends and narratives embedded within them. 'Which Hurts More?' presents the reader with a medley of tales. Sometimes Ribas's use of language is deliberately simple, while on other occasions it is rich and eloquent. Lyrical passages reflecting his country's great natural beauty are occasionally inserted at pauses in his narrative, notably in 'Damba Maria' or 'The Poor and Meek'. Prominent aspects of Angolan society, past and present, are viewed in a variety of locations, so that Kimbundu and Ovimbundu, whites and *mestiços*, traders and settlers, slavers and sorcerers, masters and servants, countryfolk, fisherfolk and townspeople all fit into a beguiling mosaic.

In short, the stories of *Echoes of My Homeland* offer a view of Angola that reflects geographical, historical, social, racial, regional and ethnic elements. Ribas offers to the world and to his own countrymen a frank and fascinating introduction to a great and emergent African nation. He died in Cascais, Portugal, on 18 June 2004, aged 95.

DAMBA MARIA

At the time the events related in this story occurred, the picturesque township of Catumbela was an important market centre for large numbers of caravans. Heavily laden with rubber, wax, ivory, honey and other regional produce, they flocked there with the object of trading with Europeans and receiving, by way of exchange, the much prized brandy, gunpowder, weapons, cloth and similar goods. But the slave trade, that shameful relic of the past, still constituted the main business, offering great profit both to the white trader and the black.

Like a sea of words, the hubbub spread out far and wide, only finally dying out as it reached into the mountains. Such was the chatter, the loud laughter, the chorus of song. The booming township was a veritable African emporium, just as Dondo had been in years gone by.

In those far-off days there lived a settler who, like so many others, had a young slave-woman as his concubine. Her story has been fondly preserved in native folklore and unfolds beneath a halo of nostalgia. Maria was her name...

She had been accustomed to the lash since puberty, and her attitude to her master was one of dog-like devotion. She didn't need to be told to do something: it was enough for him merely to conceive the wish. Yes, the wish was enough, because her body, her very life, belonged to him completely. A chattel with ragged thoughts, with tatters for a soul, what other demeanour could she present to her owner than the passive nature of the simple-minded? Just as some grasses grow short and hug the ground as though to curry its favours, so the wretched slave-girl in her cringing humility took every care to please the man who ruled her entire existence.

In spite of her condition as a slave, Maria didn't fail to mount the first rung on the ladder of progress. As a result of cohabitation, her brief loincloth was replaced by drapery, and hygiene came to fill a gap that had existed in her personal habits. Schooled by her lover, she had become extremely industrious in her housework and, like a dog scrutinizing its owner, strove hard to guess what he was thinking. So dutiful was she that he had virtually come to look upon her as though she were some kind of indispensable tool. As a result, whenever her white master went on a journey connected with his job, Maria went along with him like a benevolent shadow and usually took the water jug with her.

One afternoon, one of those many afternoons of voluptuous sunshine, someone came and knocked at the door of the house where she lived. He was a fellow-countryman of hers, yet a man of no little property, which gave him a certain respectability. He had been out hunting, but, through a reversal of roles, he had fallen victim of a dangerous foe: thirst. It was several kilometres to the town, and there were no more houses on the way there after this one. He was desperate, therefore, for a cool drink to relieve his parched tongue.

Maria answered the knock, and the stranger asked to speak to her master. But he wasn't in, he'd gone to Catumbela. Consequently, the stranger asked her for a glass of water to slake his thirst.

While the slave-girl was getting the water jug, the rich man stood there, mopping the perspiration from his face.

'Hold your hat out,' she said, a few moments later.

The stranger gaped in astonishment. 'My hat?'

'Yes, your hat,' repeated Maria serenely.

The stranger stammered out a rebuke. Did she expect him to drink out of his hat? It was all dirty with grease and sweat!

'The glass belongs to my white master, and he's the only person who may drink out of it...'

The rich man began to feel dizzy. There was a surge of anger in his chest, his eyes blazed. He could have strangled her. But he restrained himself: the woman didn't belong to him. Only her white master, her lover and owner, could punish her. He held his hat out...

Maria hesitated. The way his hand shook and his eyes flashed made her feel uneasy. Losing her courage, she stuttered: 'I'll... I'll go and get a different glass...'

'There's no need... A black man shouldn't drink out of a white man's glass... Pour it in...'

Her hands trembling with anxiety, Maria obeyed. Slowly, exasperatingly, the rich man sipped at the liquid.

However, instead of quenching his thirst, the water made him feel even hotter, for there now swelled up from the very depths of his being a new thirst, fired by the flame of hatred, the thirst for vengeance.

He made off. As he strode along, his brain seemed to be on fire. Really! Having to drink water out of his hat! Him, of all people, the owner of several farms, the master of numerous slaves! As for women, he'd no shortage of those! He had as many as ten concubines, and whenever he felt the need, all he had to do was to send for one of them! The whites shook him by the hand and treated him as a friend! Huh! Nobody had ever insulted him before! Nobody! Nobody! Not until that black woman, that backward slave, had offended him with her lack of respect, damn her!

As his mind seethed, the memory of the slave-woman's disdainful insistence rose again from the depths of temporary oblivion, like impurities boiling to the surface.

'The glass belongs to my white master, and he's the only person who may drink out of it...'

But the gall gave way to a huge smile as he suddenly exclaimed: 'You don't know me yet but you're going to!' And to give vent to his feelings, he snarled his way through his entire repertoire of obscene expletives.

The slumbering afternoon was yawning in its indolence. Still kissed by the sun's passionate rays, the trees went on lulling those who sleep in the dream of eternity, went on modulating the hymn of universal love. Dotted with clumps of vegetation, the plain stretched away, beset by the anguish of its own very solitude.

Once he reached the township, the rich man went in search of Maria's master. But he couldn't find him. For God's sake! Where could he be? If it weren't for his wanting to find him, then no doubt he'd have come across him easily. It was just too bad! Things always ran counter to his intentions! More by habit than by design, he found himself at the door of his own house.

As he crossed the yard, his workers greeted him with respectful salutes as they busied themselves with the extraction of palm oil: 'Hello, sir!'

As though enveloped in a cloud of despair, he could only grunt in reply; and when 'Old Ignoramus', his dog, welcomed him with his habitual licks, a kick sent him yelping across the yard. He showed a similar disregard for his wife, who was cooking out in the open, stumped into the bedroom and sat down at a table. He lit a pipe. As it burned away, he too mellowed along with it.

Outside, his workmen were pounding out the palm oil in twos, pum...pum, pum...pum, and chattering away noisily at the same time. In the passage, or rather, in the dining room, a canary was singing, imprisoned in its wooden cage. And there he was too, consumed with annoyance.

Chewing hard, his wife came in. 'D'you want a roasted corncob?'

Still feeling angry, however, he harshly shooed her out. 'Go away! Don't bother me!'

She grunted with scorn and went out again, muttering to herself. If he was angry, to hell with him! To think that, without being asked, she'd gone and offered him something to eat, only to be shooed out! What had *she* got to do with his business problems?

The rich man felt hot. He went over to the window.

Catumbela was bustling with activity. Amid an explosion of voices, people of both sexes were transacting business. In front of one establishment the owner was chatting to a man who had an adolescent girl at his side. Were they haggling over the sale of the girl? Possibly. At least an innocent smile revealed her happiness: the promise, no doubt, of a new dress and trinkets with which to adorn herself. Poor victim! For a few fleeting pleasures she was about to plunge for ever into the dark sorrows of slavery!

The rich man sat down again at the table. He had the glimmering of an idea. Yes, he would write to Maria's master. Perhaps he was already back home again. He picked up a pen and laboriously, ponderously, began to draw up a letter:

'Deer Mister Manuele,

Yo slayv Maria done me bad thing tooday my hart is sad. It make me neelly cry. Tooday I go by yo house den I ask a glasser water. she den ask me my at and she poot water in my at.'

'Oh, no!' he groaned and stopped writing because a particle of thread had smeared the last few letters. So as not to get his fingers all ink-stained, he wiped the nib on his hair and struggled on:

'I want by dat woman too teech her, eef yo acsep I pay yo 300 escudo. It good beeznes fo yo.'

He stopped again, but this time to read what he'd written. Yessir, very good, that was fine. And he touched up the letter by adding a few more punctuation marks.

Puffing at his pipe again, he strode up and down the room for a few moments. Suddenly, he stopped in front of a mirror. He looked at his reflection. He looked different from other men, surely! Didn't his very appearance reveal his superiority? Why did she treat him the way she did, pouring water into his hat? The barbarian! Damn slave-girl!

He went out into the yard. His workers laboured on, chattering away as usual. He went up to his wife and suddenly asked her: 'If a slave failed to show you respect, what would you do?'

His wife was sifting maize flour by banging her hand against the bottom of a wicker basket; she stopped what she was doing and gave him a puzzled look. 'I'd give him a smack... Why?'

'Oh, I was just thinking....'

He went back to the bedroom and reread his letter. He twitched his nose. He sat pondering for a few moments, then completely changed his mind. He could go along in person; that way, he'd be able to sort out any snags at once. With money you could fix anything. He screwed up the letter, put his hat on and went out.

It was growing dusk. Ever anxious for a variety of sensations, the revolving sun was heading for the other hemisphere, bent on leaving its voluptuous imprint of fertility on other parts of the world. Instead of the fervent kiss of day, there now loured the melancholy of bereavement, and, as if borne along by the evening breeze, a soothing peacefulness enveloped the earth: the birds winged their way in search of repose, the labourers in the fields could now enjoy the rewarding coolness of their own good sweat.

After a cursory inspection of the white man's customary haunts, the rich man caught sight of him heading out towards his property. 'Hi there!' he shouted.

They walked along as two equals, occasionally stopping and chatting at some length. To avoid thwarting his objective, the rich man made no reference to the water incident. He based his case for the acquisition of the slave-girl on the white settler's intended return visit to the land of his birth. Lest Maria should be sold to any one else, he was proposing to purchase her there and then. He wasn't going to haggle over the price, because he could see that she would serve him well. The settler, however, became rather sentimental and was disinclined to part with her. Eventually, the lure of money was too much for him, and he reluctantly accepted the offer. What was the point of missing such a bargain? Just because she was his woman? No, all she was, after all, was a servant. He wouldn't get anything like such a good price for her when he got back again. And so the deal was done to the satisfaction of both.

After dinner, leaning back on his canvas chair, he called the slave-girl to him and, as he puffed away at a cigarette, he explained to her, little by little, in the Umbundu language, just what he planned to do. 'You see, there's this man, a fellow-countryman of yours, who's taken a fancy to you. He wants you to go and live with him. As I've already told you before, I'm off back to my own country soon. So that you won't come to any harm while I'm away, I've arranged for you to go to him. You'll be all right, he's got plenty of money.'

Guessing who the buyer was, Maria recoiled in horror. 'You mean you've sold me?' she asked, as tears came to her eyes.

The settler coughed and stammered out the pretext that she was going to the rich man's house so that she wouldn't have to leave the area altogether.

'All right then, master. You're the one who knows best...' she said, with a sigh.

As her lover stretched out in the comfort of his chair, Maria trudged off to the kitchen, grief-stricken. There, insulated from the other servants, who were chatting out in the yard, she stood and turned the extraordinary news over in her mind. In her heart she felt that the sale was a bad omen. What was the black man's object in buying her? It couldn't be for good reasons, she'd already read that in his face. What a wretched situation to be in! And looking back along the misty path of time, she imagined herself amid people long deceased.

She pictured herself as a child in her remote village, playing with other children. By day, once she'd done her few little chores, she used to scamper about, laughing and giggling and chasing butterflies and grasshoppers. And on moonlit nights, ah! On those nights of universal gaiety, there was an unceasing round of stories and guessing games and other simple things that so amuse little children. On yet other nights, in the moonlight or by the firelight, there was singing and dancing to the accompaniment of wild, wild instruments. Afterwards, in the company of the grown-ups, she would drink maize wine, though not very much, lest she should get silly. Such happy days! Such very happy days!

One day (and what a different day that was!), one of her father's brothers called her to one side and said: 'D'you know what? I'm off on a long journey, off to where the white men live, to those places where so many people from these parts have gone to. I'd rather like you to come with me, then you could see lots of nice things: big houses... long roads... shops full of beautiful cloth, headscarves and I don't know what else... But, if you come, don't let anybody know, right?'

She agreed and off she went with him. Once they reached the place about which he'd shown such enthusiasm (it was Catumbela, where she now lived), her uncle took her along to a shop where he had a lengthy conversation with the white trader who owned it. What they said to one another, she had no idea. All she could recall, and it was as though it were happening now, was that the white man had given her a length of cloth, a headscarf and a black waistband. Finally, her uncle came up to her, placed his hand on her shoulder and, with his breath reeking of brandy, adopted an affectionate tone: 'Go and wait for me in the white man's backyard, I've still got a little more business to attend to.'

Ever so pleased with her new clothes, off she went to wait in the white man's yard. Eventually, she got tired of waiting and grew anxious at being left on her own. The day drew to an end and was followed by another and yet another. And still her uncle did not show up! At last she realized that he had tricked her: she had been sold.

Tears of rage, tears of anguish, tears springing from the very depths of her being, welled up as never before in her sorrowing eyes. Yes, she wept and wept for days on end, lamenting the fact that the man she called her uncle, her father's own brother, had sold her as though she were some prize chicken or a sucking pig. The crook! There she was, still on the threshold of life, yet robbed of her freedom! What had she done wrong that she should be punished like this? A curse on her uncle! A curse on her uncle for selling her! Accursed father! Accursed mother! A curse on her race for showing no love for its own children!

Times without number she was punished. She suffered a great deal. Then one day her master made her his woman. And yet today, for no good reason, just for money, he was selling her off as though he didn't care. Really! The very man who had plundered her innocence, the very man she so meekly served, the very man who was her lover, was just like the blacks, in spite of his white skin: he sold people too, he was just as heartless. That was gratitude for you!

And just like water babbling over the weir, Maria tearfully began to sing:

Mother of mine,
why was I born?
I was bought like a puppy,
I've been sold like a bitch.
I have no father, no mother, no brothers!...
I'm just like a silly hen
which only knows the cornmeal thrown at it...
My uncle sold me
Out of greed for money!
He sold me because he wasn't my father,
he sold me because he had no heart...

She fell silent. Just as on the very first day of her servitude, the tears welled forth with the same intensity, as though they were the lava from the fire within her soul.

When he heard her wild song, her master squirmed repeatedly on his divan: a dull irritation filled him with hatred for the wretched slave.

With increasing anguish, Maria went on:

Oh God, Father of all people,
set me free from my affliction!
Death espies me,
death awaits me,
all he needs is the command of my avenger!
Alas, mother of mine,
I'm going to die!

The man who kept her took pity on her. 'Maria!' he called.
Sobbing, she went to him.

'Why are you crying?'

Overcome with grief, she could only answer him with further tears.

'Now don't be silly! Why are you crying? Why d'you say you want to die?'

'It's my heart that tells me so, master!' she said, and she went on to relate the incident of the water.

'Aha! So you poured water into his hat? Ha! Ha! Ha! So that's why he's so struck on you and wants you to serve him with the same degree of dedication. Don't cry, you'll be all right. When you came to me, didn't you cry then too? But what about afterwards? Didn't you get used to things? Well then, the same thing will happen this time, you'll see. If I weren't so homesick for my own country, you'd have been able to go on living with me. So...'

Contrary to her habit, Maria chose to sleep in the company of the other slave-women.

'Sleeping here tonight?' said Gueve in surprise, seeing her lying there on the matting.

Maria sighed. 'Yes, I'm sleeping here for once, I'm upset and sick at heart.'

'Has the white man lost his temper with you?' inquired Zamba, spreading out another mat, on which she settled down with Gueve.

'No, he hasn't. But he doesn't love me any more. He's going to sell me.'

Although Maria's tone of voice and her very appearance revealed how sad she was, her companions found the news so absurd that they noisily voiced their doubts.

'Are you playing games with us? The white man's going to sell you? The very idea!'

'How can you talk like that, Maria?! The white man... your man... selling you?!'

Maria sat up, rested her chin on her hand and bitterly reminded them: 'But why shouldn't he sell me if he wants to? I'm a slave, aren't I? Is a slave a person? Isn't he just something to sell, like a hen or a pig or some other animal? Huh! The way you talk, anybody would think you'd forgotten you were slaves!!!'

'But it doesn't make sense; you've not done anything wrong, you've not done anything to make him want to sell you,' objected Gueve.

'My uncle sold me, didn't he? What wrong did I do him? Didn't your uncle sell you, too? What wrong did you do him? Weren't all of us slaves sold by our relatives? Yet you say the white man, who is no relative of mine, shouldn't sell me!'

There was an anguished pause in the conversation as they stopped, lost deep in thought. The sad chirping of the crickets resounded through the humble thatched kitchen. The flame of the palm-oil lamp shimmered as the wind blew in through the cracks and seemed to share in their grief. Suddenly, as though the night itself was raising its voice in lamentation, a howl rent the air.

Maria recoiled in fear, sensing an omen of death in the baleful sound. 'Oh no, I'm going to die, I can tell, I'm going to die! Mother, oh mother, why ever did you bring me into the world? There's no hope for me, there's no hope for me!'

As she burst into tears, the other two women were beset by her terror-stricken conviction. Yet they refused to abandon hope and tried all they could to calm her down.

'Don't cry, my dear, don't cry!'

'Never mind, nothing's going to happen!'

Weeping and sobbing, Maria was, nevertheless, still full of foreboding. 'Didn't you hear the dog howl?'

Gueve and Zamba soothed her as best they could.

'Oh, that's nothing, the dog only wants to get out and find some bitch for himself.'

But Maria wouldn't be convinced. 'Yes, but, don't you see, it's a sign! I already knew it in my heart! Don't think I'm crying because I've been sold, oh no! I cried the first time because I was nothing but a child. But I'm crying this time because the man who's going to buy me wants me for some evil purpose!'

Once again the dog howled, and the sound seemed to penetrate Maria's very soul. 'Dear God, sacred spirits of the dead, help me! What crime am I supposed to have committed? I've never killed anyone, I've never insulted anyone. If I've done wrong, then I implore your forgiveness at once!' As she begged, she raised her hands over her breast, joining them in prayer and then raising them to her head.

'Now, now, dear friend, don't be like that. You work very well, and your new master is bound to treat you well if you do,' said her two friends, trying to console her in her misery.

'No, that's not true! That man intends me no good!... He came here today to ask for some water, and I gave it to him in his hat... It was because the white man said he didn't want any black person to drink out of his glass...'

Meanwhile, the deep, dark night, darker than any other, rolled on, crushing the spirit of the poor slave-girl.

Next morning, the white trader was still having breakfast when a messenger arrived with a letter. 'That's a good bargain!' he reflected, with a smile difficult to describe or, at any rate, with a smile that combined niggardliness with traces of regret.

'Maria!' he called

Meekly, for all her agitation, the slave-girl appeared.

'Right then, you can be on your way now. Go with that man,' he declared, with his eyes fixed on the cup of white coffee that he was slowly stirring.

Maria did not move. There was a lump rising in her throat, and she stood there, petrified by a strange coldness that swept over her.

'I'll come and see you later when you're there, all right?' he said and, as if bewildered by her spectre-like appearance, he held out a few coppers to her.

Shocked by the apparent ignominy into abandoning her stupor, she managed to stutter a few words. 'No, thanks, master. No, thanks!' She knelt down and humbly joined her hands. 'Master, your slave Maria is leaving to join her new owner!... Good-bye, master, good-bye!'

In a daze, her ex-master followed her mechanically to the door. Leaning against the door-frame, he stood watching the two black people leave until they disappeared round a bend in the path that wound through the grass. He put his hand in his pocket to take out his tobacco. But the envelope emerged instead. Without thinking, possibly driven by the overwhelming power of greed, he counted the money again.

At length, somewhat conscience-stricken, he became irritated with the money. Mortified, he now realized how sordid his part in the deal had been. To what end had he sold her? Wasn't the devotion of that poor black girl worth much more than all the money he'd received for her? What a disgraceful way to treat her! Besides, hadn't he made use of her as his concubine?

In the mood of pity brought on by his repentance, he ordered one of his servants to go and call after Maria. But, just like the gale that piles up the clouds and then disperses them, his self-regard, welling up from the cesspool of his inner being, drove him to countermand the order. What was the point, after all? She was a slave, wasn't she? Hadn't he made similar use of other slaves? A woman? Nonsense! And anyway, it wasn't as though there were any children to hold them together! 'The blacks were born to be slaves! That's the destiny of their race! So why worry? Don't they get sent in droves to Brazil, to America, to God knows what other hell-holes?' he growled to himself. By the time he walked into his shop, whistling as he went, he had already succeeded in ridding himself of the last vestiges of pity for her.

But Maria was now far away and weeping deep down inside herself. The life of a black person was indeed a sad affair! Being sold like an animal! How could God consent to such cruelty? Didn't God like the blacks? No, indeed no! God only liked whites, they had all the luck! God didn't like blacks at all! During the night she'd implored Him constantly, but He hadn't heeded her, He'd allowed her to be sold. And what was going to become of her now? A curse on that moment when she'd given her new master that water! And it was all simply in order to carry out an order! After all, what else was she supposed to do? No, God didn't like blacks! If He did, He'd look after them better!

'Now you belong to *me*,' said the rich man in an affectionate tone, when Maria presented herself to him. 'I hope you'll serve me as well as you did your old master.'

With arms folded and eyes downcast, Maria remained silent.

'As you know', he went on, getting up from his chair, 'I enjoy hunting. So that I won't go without water, you'll be coming with me.'

When she heard this order, the slave was terrified. Oh, no! Her foreboding was going to be fulfilled. She shot him a sidelong glance. But she didn't notice anything. His facial expression betrayed no evil intention. She calmed down. Perhaps the spirits would watch over her. During the night, in heartfelt prayers, she had implored and begged and entreated. Surly they must have heard her and would now protect her.

Meanwhile, the rich man, outwardly serene, moved about the house, equipping himself with all the necessary hunting gear. 'Bring that water jug with you,' he declared, as he came to the end of his preparations.

They set out. On their way, her new master explained to her the lore of hunting. Maria was alternately worried and at ease. Was her companion seeking to deceive her? Her heart told her that he was.

The sun soared higher in the heavens; its rays beat down with a fierce ardour. No houses, no people, were to be seen. In the searing heat of noon the plain seemed lost in a deep sleep. Catumbela was left further and further behind, over the horizon.

The hunter had now fallen silent. Ablaze with a personal sun that burned within him, he walked on, meditating grimly. The slave-girl continued to bring up the rear. She was now silently weeping, as though afflicted by the wild flame that consumed his soul. Alas, the spirits were not coming to her aid! What evil had she committed to be met with such contempt? Was it because she was a slave? Alas, even they, yes, even they regarded her as an animal. As for God, He wouldn't do anything for her, either. If she was guilty of some misdeed, then why didn't they all forgive her? Why didn't they all forgive her, those beings from the Great Beyond, whatever it was that she was supposed to have done? Oh sacred spirits, oh God above, forgiveness, forgiveness, please!

'I'm thirsty. I want some water,' the rich man abruptly complained, handing her his hat.

Trembling with terror, the slave-girl could only manage to stammer: 'There's a glass here, master...'

'There's no need... I drank out of my hat yesterday as well... Don't tell me you've forgotten!' snarled the hunter, and a convulsive tremor passed from his hand to his outstretched hat.

'Forgive me, master! It wasn't my fault, the white man wouldn't allow anybody else to drink out of his glass! Those were his orders, his orders! Forgive me, can't you tell I'm crying?' She grovelled at his feet.

'You bitch!' he roared, hurling his hat into the long grass. 'At least you could have poured it into a tin can for me!' He unslung his rifle and stepped back a few paces.

With death staring her in the face, the slave-girl let out scream after scream; she tried to run away, to escape into the wilderness. But, sure and swift, an angry bullet brought her down.

'Uuuh!' moaned Maria, reaching the last step of existence.

As the shot rang out, frightened birds flew off in all directions. The killer stood and looked down at his victim for a few moments, as she lay suffering the final agonies. His face bore a profane leer, in which there mingled both exultation and terror.

'You animal! That's the last time you'll pour water into a hat!'

Quiet had once again descended on the plain. A turtle-dove began to coo. Perhaps it was the wilderness weeping.

And even today, when the train on the Benguela Railway pulls up at the Kilometre 27 halt (the place where our drama reached its climax), they call out: 'Damba Maria!' [1]

---

[1] *Damba* is an Umbundu word meaning wilderness (Translator's Note – TN).

BANGO-A-MUSSUNGO

How long ago did it happen? Nobody knows. But it is certainly beyond all doubt that the events related in this story took place long, long ago, well before the Portuguese occupation. As for the principal figure in our tale, the passing of the years has not obscured his name; echoing down the centuries, legend has kept alive the name of Bango-a-Mussungo.

He was ruler of an important region of Angola that even now bears his name; the territory he possessed was extensive, he had twelve wives and he reigned supreme over an entire people. In all things his grandeur was to be seen: in the splendour of his ostentation and in his cruelty. The news of his power spread far and wide: everyone talked about him, and their mouths gaped open in fear.

His despotic rule knew no bounds and his need to satisfy his every whim brought him close to madness. The plight of his slaves aroused not a single humane feeling within him. To him they were inferior beings, just so many animals to be treated as such. Why was this? The answer was that he came by them so cheaply. He acquired them either in exchange for the mentally retarded, or in the frequent sorties that he ordered, or as prisoners taken in successful warfare waged against other tribes. He always had plenty of people to do his bidding. Yet he utterly despised them for their abjectness. This was why, whenever he sat down or got up, he used to put all his weight on two spears that skewered their way into the hearts of two slaves lying prostrate on either side of his throne. This daily human sacrifice was consequently twice the number of times he occupied or left the royal seat. Not that this bothered him at all: there was a constant supply of replacements. Slaves were easy to come by.

Such was the depravity of this violence that his heart was never touched; deep within him, within his breast, all feeling had frozen. He never showed any sign of regret or remorse. After all, what was so special about the lives of such men? It was normal to kill oxen, pigs, chickens and other creatures. So therefore it was all right to kill men. And that was what he did, taking an immense delight in the slaughter.

Such were the fantastic whims of Bango-a-Mussungo!

It was quite extraordinary to see how his cowed subjects put up with his craziest demands. Comments never went beyond the occasional low whisper, lest he should get to know and wreak a savage vengeance. And because nobody sought to point out to him the error of his ways, the killing went on interminably: fear had struck deep into every heart. To each and every one, Bango-a-Mussungo was the Devil incarnate.

One day, after disposing of countless victims, a strange thought occurred to him: the men he killed never came back to settle their scores with him. Why? It must be because they were in a state of well-being. The other world must be preferable to this one. If their souls never came back in search of revenge, then, beyond all doubt, they dwelt in regions where they led a most desirable existence. It followed then that, once he, Bango-a-Mussungo were buried as well, he would enjoy even greater influence; he would be king of that country and would rule over its fortunate people. In that way his renown would increase, and he would gain new spheres of influence.

He pondered and meditated for a long time. And, just like the phosphorescent glow that shimmers on the sea on a dark night, his sombre meditation gave rise to the solution to the problem: he would construct an underground dwelling (three rooms and a kitchen), it would have all essential comforts, would be provided with an ample supply of food, and there below he would live, along with one of his wives and two slaves. If God held sway up above, why shouldn't he hold sway down below?

He decided that the tribal horn should be blown; he wanted to make public his resolve and to hear the views of his people. Everyone gathered under the great tree in front of his palace. The air was thick with questions. Was there going to be yet another war? Were all the slaves going to be exterminated? What could it all be about?

Flanked by his two counsellors, Bango-a-Mussungo finally appeared. He took his seat on his throne, and the two acolytes seated themselves on stools on either side of him. Then, in a deliberate, resounding voice, he proclaimed his remarkable plan.

Against the background of the great bonfires it was an awesome spectacle. The huge mass of people sitting closely side by side on the ground seemed like a colossal ant-hill. Huddled together in front of the royal mound, they listened attentively to the strange speech; from time to time parts of it were repeated by court officials.

As though from precipice to precipice they pitched from one surprise to the next, as Bango-a-Mussungo announced his scheme. No matter how hard they tried, they could make no sense of his line of argument. In low whispers they started to ask each other whether Bango-a-Mussungo had gone crazy. Their already awe-stricken faces took on even stranger looks in the glow of the leaping tongues of flame.

The spirits of his ancestors (so said Bango-a-Mussungo) had revealed extraordinary things to him: an unknown world, the underworld, a world where those who die on earth go on living. Up above, as all were well aware, there existed the world governed by God. But what none of them knew, as had been the case with him too, was that, beneath the ground, there existed another world. Let nobody have any doubts about that, because the spirits had told him. And the proof of it all lay in the fact that the dead never came back, not even to settle an old score. And why was that? The answer was that they were in a state of well-being, that they had found what they could never attain in this world. And the one who was going to reign in that other world was none other than himself, Bango-a-Mussungo. What he was saying, as they would do well to believe, was no crazy dream; it was a great truth, vouchsafed to him by his ancestors. He had pondered long on it, by day and by night. At long last he had made up his mind; it was his duty to accept the task revealed to him, he had all along been the chosen one; assuredly he was the first man predestined for such a mission. Why? He had no idea. Perhaps it was because of his great talent, or possibly it was on account of his great courage. At all events, whatever the reason, he had been chosen to govern that strange world. God would continue to hold sway in Heaven, whilst down below it would be he who would rule supreme. For that reason, he was going to give orders for the construction of an underground dwelling.

While he was making his speech, a cold and awesome quiet had fallen over his audience. From the very outset the same question nagged at everyone's mind: had Bango-a-Mussungo gone crazy? Whether he had or not, his rascally counsellors were plainly in support of his scheme. They expressed approval of his being chosen king of that other world and hastened to agree that the fingers of his ancestors pointed to this conclusion.

With the support of his ministers, his people ventured into the same treacherous agreement with him; they burst into applause, showered warm congratulations on him and wished him a reign of great splendour.

Overjoyed, Bango-a-Mussungo thanked them for their effusive congratulations and promised to be a great king, even better than he was already. As was the practice, libations of fermented honey, served in gourds to the assembled multitude and in a great jar to the tribal chief and his courtiers, celebrated the beginning of this extraordinary undertaking.

On the following day he sent for men and started to issue orders. A huge hole began to be excavated. The royal quarters took shape, and the residence of Bango-a-Mussungo caused everybody to experience a sense of growing amazement. Nobody could believe what they saw. It was all like some incredible dream or some strange drunken stupor. But everybody looked forward to the completion of the work; on no account should Bango-a-Mussungo be steered away from his objective; he was the focal point of a deep, deep loathing.

Gems sparkled in the velvet night sky. Pounding in feverish delight, a great festival filled the terraces of the tribal palace. It was Bango-a-Mussungo's farewell.

His people were drunk twice over: drunk with joy and drunk with liquor. They staggered wildly through a seemingly unending series of dances, shouting hoarsely and giving private thanks for that strange moment that gave birth to his obsession. Men and women, both young and old, swirled round and round in dizzy pleasure. The drums and hornpipes played in a great frenzy. It was like the middle of a huge storm.

By the light of the blazing pyres weird shadows jerked to and fro in time with their owners, doubling the number of dancers. The enjoyment went on and on, everything was wonderful; and, seated happily on his throne, Bango-a-Mussungo beamed at the excited crowd...

All around, the jungle throbbed, as though taking part in the festivities; the foliage sang, and the tall fronds danced; the wind played honeyed scales, and the surroundings were imbued with infinite religious mystery. But the revellers, growing more and more intoxicated, were oblivious of the woodland concerto; the crescendo of noise: the singing, the raucous laughter, the constant hubbub of voices, the whining of the hornpipes, the pounding of the drums, all combined to drown any sounds other than those of the revelry. Yet one who could hear nature's orchestra in all its poetry was Bango-a-Mussungo. In order to bid a last farewell to earthly love, he had swallowed a love-potion and, whenever his licentious gaze fell upon some tempting beauty, he would eagerly slip away with her to a favourite corner of the thicket.

In those unique moments his soul parted from his languid body and, borne aloft on the wings of his obsession, made pilgrimage into a magical land. On their fleeting visits to this romantic bower, Bango-a-Mussungo and persons unnamed were able to listen to the great symphony of the forest.

The watchfires, with logs ablaze, flamed vigorously upwards, gleefully crackling. Their crimson light illuminated the entire festive circle and contributed greatly to the crowd's enthusiasm. Flickering unceasingly, the tongues of fire swirled in mad confusion; just like the thronging people and the leaves of the great forest, they joined in the joyous revelry. The smoke spiralled heavenwards, mingling with the blackness of the night sky. The glow from the fire, alive with writhing, mirthful shapes, radiated its splendour over the festive company, redoubling the number of those present with the shadows that it threw.

Night was drawing to its close, its bright jewels were fading into the mystery of the firmament. In the east the sombre nocturnal vestments were giving way to the gay apparel of dawn. A soft light, gentle as a mother's kiss, stole across the heavens. Sparrows, parakeets and other winged songsters were now stirring from their nests; their busy discordant choir paid homage to the infant day. Joyfully, amorously, the turtle-doves crooned a heartfelt rhapsody.

Meanwhile, the thronging crowd danced on, stamping their feet in growing frenzy. But no longer were they impelled by sheer enjoyment, now there was a nervous expectancy: suppose he were to change his mind? Anxious to flatter him, they saluted him, crying out: 'Congratulations, oh great Bango-a-Mussungo! May you be as great in the other world! May the spirits protect you!'

Their demonstrations of adulation were accompanied by the eruption of great joy on every face; on every side were rapturous smiles...

The long-awaited moment arrived. At a command from Bango-a-Mussungo, the court usher brought the revels to a close with a blast on the great ox-horn. Humbly, with deep anxiety clutching their hearts, they all seated themselves on the ground before their lord.

'All of you, counsellors and people, all of you now listening to me, I want you to concentrate on what I am about to say. Every day, are you all listening?... every day I want all of you to visit me at my new residence. Nobody must be absent, the king's wish is an order!' So demanded Bango-a–Mussungo as he stood there, panting with excitement. Spontaneously, with one mighty voice, his subjects swore to obey. No longer troubled by their first worry, they accompanied him in one huge retinue.

Frenzy galvanized every heart. Could it really be true? Was Bango-a-Mussungo really going to go down into the hole, just as if he were being buried, as though already dead? It had to be seen to be believed! The truth could be read on his face, of course, but perhaps his heart was concealing a lie. Ah! But if he was really going to bury himself!...

In a last act of homage the ministers addressed speeches to their chief; they hailed him as the favourite son of the tribal gods, they wished him a successful reign in his new, mysterious world. In an act of deification a great chorus of voices went up from the multitude; like a plea for redemption it soared up to heaven; like a great entreaty it echoed from hut to hut, throughout the whole township. And Bango-a-Mussungo, in great excitement, made his way down into the cavern, followed first by his chosen wife and then by his slaves. An enormous flat stone, like a mighty door, closed the entrance to the new royal chambers.

The following morning, all his people made their way to the new royal domain. One of his counsellors, banging on the stone, inquired of him through an airhole: 'Bango-a-Mussungo, Bango-a-Mussungo, how have things been down there?'

'Not too bad... The only thing I don't like is the darkness.'

On the second day, the pilgrimage was repeated. Once again, just as on the day before, the counsellor asked: 'Bango-a-Mussungo, Bango-a-Mussungo, how have things been down there?'

'Well, things aren't quite as I imagined. I'm already getting a bit bored. If things continue like this, I shall come back to be with you all again.'

The people all looked at one another, there were muttered exchanges, and one thought spontaneously occurred to everybody: they must prevent Bango-a-Mussungo from getting out. Spreading like an epidemic, there was an outbreak of all sorts of antics: they pulled faces, made rude gestures and grunted abusive remarks. Nobody wanted him as king any longer; their discontents had given rise to a deep hatred for him.

Parents had lost their children, children had lost their parents, wives had lost their husbands. And why? Because Bango-a-Mussungo lived for the sight of bloodshed, killing was a way of life for him. So, who needed him, then? Nobody! As he had sown evil, evil was what he should reap.

Now that he was below ground, below ground let him receive his due reward. That was what he had wanted. Let him suffer, therefore, the heavy blow his own hands had prepared.

How could they show any pity for Bango-a-Mussungo, if he had never taken pity on anybody? No, he must remain in that hole of his, his new residence must now serve as his tomb. Everybody was weary of his acts of cruelty, for so long they had waited for him to die, and now that the longed-for moment had arrived, were they going to go to his aid, to prolong his life? No! Parents had lost their children, children had lost their parents, wives had lost their husbands.

Whenever it suited him, he would take other men's wives, and, instead of being hanged, as tribal tradition demanded, whenever a king committed such an offence, this fate befell the wretched husband who was unwise enough to protest. His forebears had done the same thing, admittedly, but he had exceeded them by far. Because of the fear he inspired, he did whatever he thought fit. Why did anyone need him? Let him stay in that grave of his to reign over the dead! With that, they blocked up the airhole.

On the third day, the multitude, more interested than ever, made a further pilgrimage to the royal tomb. Unblocking the airhole, the same courtier as before repeated his usual question: 'Bango-a-Mussungo, Bango-a-Mussungo, how have things been down there?'

A desperate wail reached their ears: 'Aargh! I can't go on living down here any longer! Take away that stone, I want to come out or I'll die! We're exhausted from shouting for help, but nobody answered! Aargh, quickly, take away that stone, I feel I'm going to die!'

As an answer, they blocked up the opening again, and before the strange inmates could revive, they piled boulders on top.

On the next pilgrimage, not a sound could be heard. They judged by the silence that Bango-a-Mussungo's new reign had already begun...

This state of affairs did not entirely dispel their anxiety; they were still afraid that his soul, beyond all doubt now transformed into a demon, would break down the heavy stone over the entrance. To settle their fears, they heaped more and more stones on top until they had formed a megalithic monument. This has now disappeared, owing to man's destructive nature, and all that is left is the original stone.

How long ago did it happen? Nobody knows. But it is certainly beyond all doubt that the events related in this story took place long, long ago, well before the Portuguese occupation. As for the principal figure in our tale, the passing of the years has not obscured his name; echoing down the centuries, legend has kept alive the name of Bango-a-Mussungo.

PEOPLE OF THE SEA

It is still night. The roosters are already beginning to crow. Awakened by these unique nocturnal clocks, the three fishermen make their way down to the sea, to face another day's toil. They are each wearing a singlet, with a smock down to their knees and a roll of cloth around their heads. Impelled by sturdy arms, a canoe is dragged into the water and, with oars plying, it wends its way out into the open sea.

The lines are cast. The two older men, Sebastião and Domingos, light up their clay pipes. And, as they smoke, they ponder on life and at intervals haul out a huge fish.

High, high above, the stars proclaim the Great Beyond; beneath them the sea gives spiritual expression to the sorrows of the world; all around them, the solitude makes itself felt, meditative and oppressive.

Agostinho, a young man of about twenty, was lost in tender memories: thoughts of Teresa had sprung up in his mind, alluring, inflaming him as he recalled her dark, dark eyes. Ecstatically he savoured the promises of love she had made, he savoured her whims, her little jealousies, the whole microcosm of sweet nothings that captivate the heart. Occasionally he took a deep breath, as though inhaling not only the sea air, but also great draughts of happiness. Unlike his companions, sagely nodding over their lines, the light of his soul shone out of him in a rapturous smile.

Gently soughing the whole time, the sea rocked him to and fro in his delight.

With inexpressible excitement he recalled the conversation they had had a few hours before he went to bed. He could still hear her leisurely voice giving the details of what she had acquired that day. The linen, the pans, the plates, other small things, the lot, yes, she'd already bought the lot. Fortunately, he had already made the traditional donation to her family: Neptune, that generous giant, had provided everything he had needed for the purpose. For his future well-being, his father had presented him with a canoe. And so, the very next day, he was going to set up home with Teresa.

Because of recent turbulent seas, Teresa didn't want him to go fishing. The sea is treacherous; that is what she had told him that very night. It provided their food, yes, but it also killed people. Whether they were its children or not, the sea, alas, cared not a bit. He ought to stay away from it, not be so stupid as to go and get killed. After all, he did want to set up house with her, didn't he? 'Can't you just do this one thing I want? I don't want to be a poor widow! D'you hear what I say, my love?' So she pleaded, languidly leaning her head against his shoulder.

As for Agostinho, though he was pleased to hear her urgent entreaties, he made light of her fears. Die? Ha! Ha! Ha! She shouldn't make him laugh! Did she mean to imply that the sea, his friend, would kill him just like that, for no reason? What crime had he committed that he should suffer such a misfortune? No, the sea liked him, it wouldn't do him any harm. Wasn't it thanks to the sea that they'd got to know each other? And it would be the sea that would provide a souvenir of their betrothal: with the profits from his fishing, he'd buy her a pair of gold earrings. She'd see. 'There's no point in arguing! I'm going all the same. I want to try out my new canoe,' he added vehemently, giving her chin a gentle tug.

Teresa went on insisting that he shouldn't go out fishing, that she was speaking with a heavy heart. But Agostinho refused to give way and chided her for her gloominess. 'Just don't cry, d'you hear?' And off he went, satisfied that he was getting his own way.

A deep sigh escapes him. On the wings of his imagination, he travels back through time. It is early morning; he finds himself on the opposite shore of the estuary. Here and there canoes floated at rest. In the blue heavens wild ducks were in full throat, descending at intervals to seize small fish in their great beaks. The harsh cries of ravens echoed from the tops of the lofty coconut palms, which reared up, in small clumps, as marker trees for the various fishing communities. The ocean rolled gently on, intoning its ceaseless lament. Like so many seagulls, several girls were out in quest of mussels. They resembled birds scratching in the sand as they dug around in it, until finally they nimbly located the elusive molluscs. They let out intermittent cries of triumph and sometimes had to scamper after the shellfish as the tide swept them away from their outstretched hands. Constantly scuttling about, they gleefully built up and added to their haul, which they could later hawk around the streets of the great city of Luanda.

Amid all the work and bustle, Teresa gradually became separated from the main group of her friends. The gracefulness of her body was accentuated by the bending and swooping of her task. A darting of the feet was followed by a plunging of the hands; she squatted down here, shifted over there; she beamed in triumph whenever she stopped one of the creatures from getting away. She fascinated Agostinho. Though he'd seen her often enough before, he was so overcome with love that he could have eaten her. He approached her flirtatiously. 'Aha! God seldom gives us what we most want! If only I could be the sea and give you a whole pile of shellfish!'

Without even looking him in the face, she answered him as she went on with her task: 'Eh? Would you just give me some shellfish? Nothing else as well?'

'Well, plenty of fish too... I'd give you everything so you could go and buy nice clothes, gold earrings, bracelets, anything you wanted!'

'And couldn't you offer me all that as a man anyway?' taunted Teresa, now looking straight at him.

Hesitating as he chose his words, Agostinho stammered: 'Only if you were my wife...'

'Ha! Ha! The man who thinks he can court me must first appear to me in a dream!'

'Well, in that case, I'm the one you're going to be dreaming about...'

'Eh? Now look what a mess I'm in!'

'Don't scoff at the idea. Your heart will tell you it's true, and the heart is never wrong. Just you wait and see.'

But, with a torrent of giggles, Teresa left her poor gallant standing on his own, his eyes following her with a lovesick gaze.

The next day, just when Teresa was leaving to sell her wares, with her basket balanced on her head, Agostinho was ready in wait for her. His greeting found greater expression in the movement of his eyes than in the words he uttered. 'Well then, did you dream about me?'

'Really! Don't bother me! Do you think I've nothing better to do than dream of you?' she retorted, with a grumpiness that gave way to a more pleasant manner.

Days went by, and each day he asked her the same question: 'Well then, did you dream about me?' His constant questioning sought to soften the firmness of her denials.

But eventually, after the habitual answer, when she had gone a few more steps, she turned back and called after him. 'Yes, I've dreamed about you...'

And thereafter, under the auspices of the celestial minstrel, they both dreamed the same dream every night.

One of the old men belches and wheezes.

A damp wind blows funereal kisses. And the ocean, resembling a zebra's back in motion, with an alternation of white stripes and fiery patches, went on moaning and shuddering unceasingly. The night grieved as it hung over the vast watery wilderness.

At the sound of the belching and wheezing, the magical thread of Agostinho's thoughts suddenly snaps. 'Aha! The sea's getting angry!' he says, with a hint of anxiety in his voice.

Knocking out his pipe on the side of the boat, Sebastião, who is in fact Agostinho's father, breaks in. 'Oh, it's been like this for days now...'

'Anyway, you get a better catch when it's rough,' says Domingos, in a tone just like his partner's.

Tucking his pipe away in his satchel, Sebastião comments: 'Yes, you get a better catch, but it's more dangerous. What good is it to have a chance of catching more fish, if we have to risk death to get them? Hah! We have to earn money the hard way!'

'Yes, but whether you put to sea or stay at home, you've got to die some time. The man who's afraid just doesn't make any money. Your belly needs food, your family needs clothes, you have to pay your district licences,' Agostinho retorts, remembering the objections he made to Teresa earlier.

'Bah! You're still a boy yet! If you'd had some of the frights I've had, you wouldn't talk like that!'

'If this swell goes on like this,' opines Domingos, breaking off from his pipe, 'we'll have to summon up the sea-wizard,[1] just as we've had to

---

[1] The sea-wizard, or *kilamba* in Kimbundu, has the role of interpreting the feelings of the mermaid and of placating her anger (TN).

before. The mermaid must be angry with us. If we're going to calm her down, we'll have to give her quite a party!'

'Angry with us, no! It's not our fault, we've not wronged her in any way. The whites have, yes, they're the ones to blame. Why did they have to go and smash the rocks where she used to live?'

'The rocks on the other side of the fort, near the bridge?' asks Agostinho, full of curiosity.

'That's right. It was on those rocks that the sea-wizard used to lay a table for her. He spread a mat, covered it with a new cloth and would set out all kinds of choice dishes for her: white people's food and black people's food. As for the wines, ah, there was every kind of wine as well! Red wine, white wine, port, brandy, maize wine, palm wine, all served in all manner of new glasses. As for the cutlery, that too was always new. Oho! We really saw to it that she stayed pleased with us! She really was, too, she even did this...' and he clicked his fingers. 'I heard it with my very own ears. If anybody had told me so, I wouldn't have believed it. But I heard it, I really did.' He banged his chest with his fist. 'It's because the whites don't believe in anything that they're now paying for their audacity.'

Domingos, who was supporting the story with monosyllabic grunts, now goes on to develop it. 'That's right, damn them! Now they're paying for it, it's all their fault. And when blood shot out of the rocks, wasn't that why?'

Agostinho is surprised. 'D'you mean the rocks actually bled?'

'They did indeed and quite a lot too. Has nobody ever told you about it? That blood must have been the mermaid's tears,' answered his father, with clear conviction.

'The white men's punishment is that they're going to lose the island. It's breaking up, piece by piece.'

'And it's all going to disappear, just like the rocks did.'

'Exactly! The whites don't believe in things the blacks believe in, for them it's all lies... Yet if it weren't for the sea-wizard, who dived down to implore the mermaid, would they have been able to build the bridge across?'

'Hardly! A fine dance they'd have been led! The bridge would always be falling down...'

'So that's what happened?' exclaims Agostinho.

Domingos spits hard. 'But what do the whites know about anything?' he declares. 'Look, my wife Ximinha really knows about these things, she's seen the mermaid with her own two eyes.'

Full of conviction and with a hint of fear in his voice, he goes on to relate an episode to prove the existence of such beings. It took place at the mouth of the River Kwanza, on the Kissama side. Ximinha was sitting with the water up to her waist and enjoying a very pleasurable bathe. Slowly, gently, she began to doze. She could see and hear everything; she had merely lost the mobility of her limbs. As though she were in a dream, a mysterious voice addressed her. 'Get out of the water. There's a crocodile about, and he'll get you.'

Awaking from her doze, Ximinha tried to run. But she couldn't. She was unable to move. Suddenly, a little old black woman, as tiny as a three-year-old child, arose before her from the bottom of the river. She was dressed in a length of cloth smeared in a mixture of palm oil and tacula dye.[2] Around her waist she wore a cord made from fibres of the baobab tree. The ends of the cord opened out in a sort of fringe, one hanging at the front and the other at the back. Around her shoulders she had a shawl, consisting of another length of cloth treated in the same way, but decorated with a cross made of white ribbon, in the centre of which there stood out a little row of white, black and red beads, rounded

---

[2] The tacula tree (*Pterocarpus tinctorius*) is a native Angolan tree, much valued both for its timber and for its reddish dye (TN).

off by an aquatic almond. From her head, which was likewise smeared in palm oil, great tresses hung down. Dangling from her neck were three strings of beads similar to the others, a cross fastened to a red ribbon and two amulets: a small bag and a small idol.

This strange woman, who was a servant of Mutakalombu, the god of aquatic animals, pulled Ximinha onto dry land. Immediately, a crocodile reared its head from the water and was on the point of lunging forward to seize her. But it lost its balance, fell back and was lost from view. Mutakalombu didn't want the crocodile, his 'dog', to attack Ximinha.

In her panic, Ximinha had at last regained control of her limbs and she headed off into the distance. Either out of diffidence or for some other reason, she failed to tell anybody of the incident. Indeed, shortly after, she revealed an even greater lack of prudence, when, on the invitation of some friends, she once more went for a bathe.

Now the truth is that Ximinha did not know how to swim. Unexpectedly, the current began to carry her away. At one point she was swept under and then, shortly after, was borne to the surface again.

People ran to lend a hand, the moment her companions yelled out. Fishermen dashed to help, some swimming, some in canoes, all anxiously bent on rescuing her. Ximinha was brought back, unable to move or to speak but at peace in her heart.

In spite of all efforts to revive her, Ximinha failed to respond. Finally, she fell into a deep sleep. In her sleep there appeared Nongwene, who was the mermaid who held sway over that side of the river and was the wife to Kabula-Kaombu, the water sprite from the opposite bank. She was white, beautiful, of average stature, and her blonde hair reached down to her ankles. She was also dressed in white. She approached, full of smiles, accompanied by two black handmaidens who also wore white. After greeting Ximinha, she seated herself on a fur-covered stool that one of her handmaidens made ready for her. It gleamed with studs, and beneath it there nestled a little dog.

'What a pretty girl! Perhaps she ought to live with us down below! Do you want to come with us? Our mistress is very kind...' said one of them.

But the other immediately broke in: 'No, young woman, don't come. Just you stay put with your mother.'

'Why shouldn't she come? Didn't we leave our mothers? Come on, my dear, you come with us. Down there we've got everything.'

'Don't be tempted, my dear. Down below we're half people and half fish.'

Their mistress spoke not a word but just went on smiling a beautiful smile.

So as to win the dispute, the other handmaiden stretched out her hand: 'Never mind what she says. Just come along with us.'

Ximinha was in the act of giving her her hand but was prevented from doing so by a sudden push. She screamed. And with her scream there returned her power of speech.

'That must have been the mermaid, come to carry you off!' explained one of those watching over Ximinha. 'Tell us about it tomorrow. Something untoward could happen just now. Night is not the right time for relating such things.'

The men fall silent.

The sea is getting rougher and rougher. As though in a fearful attack of epilepsy, it is now foaming abundantly, spattering the air with great flecks of saliva. Its voice, profoundly changed, explodes in curses, in guffaws, in moans. Just like humanity in despair, it reveals its own perversity, ground beneath the heel of time.

The three fishermen withdraw their lines. Beneath the pallor of dawn, they head for land. The canoe, driven on by the violence of the surf, advances, shuddering with fear.

Close to the shore, the two older men, afraid of the pounding breakers, plunge into the water. Agostinho, however, reacts in a different manner. He catches sight of Teresa, who, along with other people, worried by the roar of the waves, had rushed down to the sea to witness the return of the fishermen. Smiling, he waves to her as though to say 'Never fear, the sea is my friend'. In this way he wanted to show her how intrepid he was. But what folly, what vanity! A much angrier wave picks up the little craft and hurls him downward, enveloping him, sucking him beneath the canoe. There is a fiery outburst of screams, the air is rent by entreaty.

'Aah! Gana zambi, gana zambi! (God help us, God help us!)'

Terrible moments of apprehensive waiting! In stricken reaction, every heart falters as every eye strains.

While the two older fishermen, especially the father, swim with the greatest urgency, other fishermen attempt to rescue him from on land. Every effort is useless! Forced under by the canoe, the grievously battered Agostinho was already a corpse.

The amorous dream that every day the sea was wont to colour with hopes was now coloured in sombre hue, casting its shadow across Teresa's soul.

Oh fickle sea, quell your rage and lament your madness. As long as you behave violently, you will not cease to suffer. Remorse will constantly pursue you. Why must you fill with mourning the hearts of those who seek protection in you? Why do you foster dreams, only to stifle them later? Listen: can't you hear their curses? Ah! They matter nothing to you! Weep, then, for ever!

Next day, in his humble coffin, transported in a canoe, the hapless bridegroom is borne to the cemetery for burial. By way of final homage, a fleet of similar craft accompanies the funeral canoe as it heads out across the bay... The sea, perhaps now contrite, laments soulfully, adding its plaints to the plaints of the mourners.

THE THIEF AND THE SORCERER

Where? In the Kissama region. In what district? In the part ruled over by Chief Kimone Kya Songa. And when did this episode take place? A long, long time ago, at least one hundred and fifty years past.

Beneath the ceremonial tree, within that palace precinct that serves as an area both for the tribal council and for recreation, men were often to be found busy at their work, listening to the honeyed words of the storytellers. Holding court in their midst, the chief enjoyed the pleasant way in which day followed day and enjoyed too the spiritual solace that this sheltered existence conferred upon him.

One day, the sorcerer Shambeje put a question to those who were present: 'Of the sorcerer and the thief, which is the first one to go out at dead of night?'

Nobody answered, and they all cautiously pretended to be very involved with their work. What was the point of answering? How did they know whether or not this was some sort of trick? No, they weren't going to take risks where serious matters were concerned, they'd no wish to throw away their lives for nothing. Who could possibly know what went on in somebody else's mind?

'Is it not the sorcerer?' went on Shambeje.

Instinctively Kamukolo could contain himself no longer. 'What do you mean, the sorcerer! It's the thief.'

'Oho! So the thief goes out before the sorcerer, does he?'

'Yes, at the time the thief is about, there's no sign of the sorcerer.'

'Let's have a bet on it, then. And all you gentlemen can judge which of us is right.'

But their listeners unanimously rejected such a suggestion. No, they couldn't say anything. Only the sorcerer and the thief understood such matters.

Like a tomb opening, a great silence fell over this unwelcome discussion. Nearby, from the harem, mingling with the thudding of the men's hammers, there issued the sound of women's voices, and snatches of their song sweetened the air. Under the caress of the sun's rays, the trees resounded with the chirring of the cicadas, and the bell-like calling of the birds embraced the whole forest in a vast and fervent hymn of praise. Shouting and laughing, a gang of children, of whom the smallest were completely naked, frolicked through the long grass. Some were chasing locusts, whose wings and legs they pulled off, before sticking them inside small pumpkins, prior to their being finally cooked in palm oil (how delicious!). Other children, especially the boys, made off further, clambering aloft to the treetops, to return triumphant with the contents of nests, or even lay in wait till a tiny turtle-dove fell into one of their traps. Here and there, either alone or with their young, were pigs and hens, goats and oxen, all peacefully grazing. Clad in skirts of slender fabric and with bangles around their ankles, women made their way to and fro, carrying baskets and water jars. Men went by too, wearing wide aprons, with M-shaped wires through their nostrils, and carrying spears, machetes or bundles of firewood. To give them a unified appearance, they all had their hair smeared with palm oil mixed with tacula dye, so that it was like scarlet coral at the tips. To give them all a fine note of distinction as well, their canine teeth and incisors were all filed to sharp points.

'Hi, Bebeka,' the chief suddenly called out to one of his concubines, who was also passing by with her bundle on her back and her child riding astride her shoulders. 'Why have you been so long?'

The woman approached and greeted those present by clapping her hands together. 'Ah, it's morning at last, gentlemen.' And she gave a great yawn. 'I've been hearing, my lord, all about what happened yesterday to Kanjila's grandchild, the one that's possessed.'[1]

'Really? And what *did* happen?'

'I've still got to deliver this water jar, my lord.'

'No, just a moment. Tell us about it right now, or otherwise our *kilamba* won't rest till he's heard about it all...'[2] And, with that, he gesticulated roguishly in the direction of that member of his court who specialized in such occult matters. Already seized by curiosity, the latter had left off his more humdrum job of making rope from baobab fibres.

Smiling yet submissive, the woman laid her child on the ground, as well as the water jar that she was carrying on her back, suspended from her head by a stout cord. Once she had shed her burdens, she squatted down respectfully, not forgetting to arrange neatly the tassels of her dress before she did so.

'You know, of course, my lord,' she said modestly, 'that Kanjila has a grandson who was born possessed.'

'Yes, that's true. I remember he asked for something to eat, the moment he emerged from the womb,' broke in the *kilamba* by way of corroboration.

---

[1] The child in question is possessed by a *kituta* (a Kimbundu word), a spirit that allegedly shares the child's body in common with the child's own personality. This is often accompanied by physical deformity (TN).

[2] This particular *kilamba* is a specialist in the occult and spiritual world, a man gifted in interpreting the actions of a *kituta*. His alleged powers are related to rain-making, to warding off wild beasts and to protecting his village from adversity in general (TN).

The chief nodded. 'Yes, yes, I've heard the story. Wasn't that the only time he asked?'

'That's right. After that, time was left to run its course. The *kituta* was quite satisfied to have made its point, which the family, naturally, had understood.'

'Yes, and as the child grew up,' said the woman, taking up her story again and gently rotating the bangles that encircled her ankles, 'all he wanted was his grandmother, Kanjila. Neither his father nor his mother was of any real importance to him, but, if anyone were to take ~~to take~~ his grandmother from him, they'd have robbed him of everything. If his grandmother went off to the stream, he used to cry and wanted to go along as well; if she went to someone's house, he'd cry because he wanted to go too. And so, wherever his grandmother went, her grandson always had to go with her. Even when she went working in the fields. And off they'd go, the two of them. Yesterday (you already know, noble lord, what our old people are like), the grandmother refused to go and work in the fields with her grandson, she just didn't feel up to it. "Don't you want to take me?" the child bawled at her. "If you don't, the buffaloes will come and appear to you during the night!" The old woman wasn't bothered by this and just chuckled to herself. But, oh, noble lord! The things that child came out with next, one wouldn't expect them even from a grown-up.'

'But, seeing that the child is possessed by a *kituta*, why didn't his grandmother pay more heed?' queried the *kilamba*, in a reproachful tone.

The chief expressed the same feeling. Quite so, she shouldn't have done what she did, she knew perfectly well what her grandson was.

'That's right, noble lord,' the woman went on. 'Just as the child said, at night, the buffaloes came and surrounded the house, making their mournful noises. And they did this despite the bonfires that are supposed to keep wild animals away. The poor old woman was terror-stricken and started shouting and screaming. People who had been sleeping in nearby plantations got up and went to see what it was all about. But nobody went too close. Instead, they called out from a great distance. " What's going on, Kanjila? What's happened to you?" and she begged them to get her grandson. "If you don't, the buffaloes will kill me!" And so they scampered off to get her grandson. But he was already awake and was calling out to his parents: "Aha! Now my grandmother's crying, the buffaloes won't leave her house alone!" So they took the child along. And the buffaloes went away.'

'There's no doubt about that child being possessed by a *kituta*,' the *kilamba* declared.

The chief gave a wave of his hand and good-humouredly added, 'Off you go now, Bebeka, our *kilamba* is now quite satisfied.'

Humbly clapping her hands together as before, she slowly got up and took her leave, once again re-arranging the thick fringe of tassels on her dress. She picked up both the water jug and her little boy, who was playing with handfuls of earth.

'As long as people do what the child's *kituta* wants, then there'll be a great future for our *kilamba*, noble lord,' observed the high priest.

'Indeed there will, indeed there will. What happened yesterday really is a great sign,' said the chief, in clear agreement.

'Merely in what he says, he'll tower above us all! So that, when he's hungry and has no food in the house, don't you see how the *kituta* will send him some? The *kituta* will simply say: "Grandmother, go down to the stream and fetch back some food for me." Oh, yes, noble chief, he'll be a great *kilamba*! But I don't know how the family is going to sort out its problems.'

'What problems?' asked the chief in surprise.

'Do you mean you haven't heard what the *kituta* has asked for?'

'No, I know nothing about it…'

'Well, it's asked for a couple of children. And who is going to hand their child over just like that? Now, if it were a question of a goat or a pig or even an ox...'

'Really, is that so? The *kituta* wants a couple of children? Well, certainly, nobody is going to hand children over freely. The only way would be for the *kituta* to go and get them...'

'Everybody knows it doesn't kill anybody, it merely takes the person off to where it lives. But to hand one's child over of one's own free will, I agree, nobody will do that.'

With one eye pensively closed and his right hand stroking his goatee beard, the chief mused: 'If the family has the resources, let it buy two children; and, if it hasn't, then it ought to put out a fibre tray for donations. Surely, that way, it should be able to buy them; one person will give one thing, another person will give something else, a third person will contribute something different still and so on... what do you think of the idea?'

'Yes, I like it. That way, the two parents won't actually have any personal involvement with the children who are to be bought.'

They fell silent. Under the great shade of the ceremonial tree, the assembled company went on sitting round, either on the ground or on stones, forever busy with the fashioning of idols, spoons, gourds, combs, rush matting, ropes, arrows, spears and deerskin bags. A low murmur of voices began to be heard as they chatted about the news. Beyond them, urchins could be heard enjoying the spectacle of a monkey, tethered by a rope, attacking a sow that had wandered in its direction. But, to settle the anomaly, a dog leapt at the monkey, barking and biting with all its might.

An elder, who had only just arrived, walked slowly and steadily forwards, holding his pipe firmly to his mouth with his right hand, while his left hand kept on twisting and twirling the skirts of his garment, as though he were deep in thought. Finally, in a voice that old age had robbed of its vigour, he saw fit to give his opinion: 'If that child really has such power, then why don't we call a meeting to ask him to make it rain? There's been a lot of activity so far, but we've had very little rain in recompense. You don't suppose the *kituta* is angry with us?'

'I'd already had the same thought,' said the *kilamba*, in a tone of approval, 'but I was waiting for others to speak first. It really is a fact that I derive a lot of power from the *kituta* myself. It seems to me that what we should do at this stage is to persuade the father to get his son to ask the *kituta*. I've already done all I can, but it doesn't appear to be hearing me too well.'

'Well, if that's the general opinion,' broke in the chief, 'then the father must be spoken to about the idea. If he says yes, then I'll ask my counsellors if they wish to be associated with the entreaty. At any rate, their own efforts have produced very little rain so far.'

The *kilamba* answered him with enthusiasm: 'You too have the making of a great *kilamba*! And now people must help the parents to provide the two children that the *kituta* requires!'

Kimone Kya Songa stood up and smoothed down his long-sleeved tunic. 'So be it, then. We'll have to get it all fixed. This child is not only a source of great honour for his parents, but also for the whole tribe.' And, with that, the chief took his leave, swirling his robe around him as his skirts swung from his waist.

'Shall we be going?' asked Shambeje anxiously. Deep in the shadows of that very same night, four figures advanced with quiet and measured tread.

'I'm out at night. Am I crazy?' they kept repeating in sinister fashion.

The village slept. They were observed only by the grim darkness of the night, their protector and accomplice. Darkness brought shudders to bird and beast alike and was a constant threat to the few creatures still abroad. Silent yet sharp, the wind was on the prowl, ready to strike anguish into the hearts of the unrighteous. But none of this hindered evil deeds, in fact it facilitated them; terror has to do with the soul and with the spiritist exercises of the magicians.

'Where was he buried, then?' asked one of the group, in a low voice.

Another one answered, kicking his foot against a mound of soft earth: 'Right here. Didn't you come to his funeral today?'

With satanic glee ('Up you come, corpse, show yourself!'), Shambeje and an accomplice oversaw the exhumation of the dead man, who lay placidly stretched out on a mat; they completed the operation by sprinkling the ground with special powder.

Nearby, so that the grave should be guarded with maximum security, dwelt the dead man's relatives, who were now asleep, resting from their efforts to find solace. But they couldn't hear anything; sorcerer's work escapes the attention of everybody.

'He's ours now!' exclaimed one of the others, as they placed the body on a litter. Shambeje's partner or, rather, his assistant in sorcery, broke in to add, with similar malice: 'Indeed he is, both body and soul!'

Striding swiftly away, they set off to carry out their strange ritual. Of what consequence was it to them that the grave should have been broken open? Let the family get the medicine man to help them in their suspicions...

'We're late this time!' said Shambeje, anxiously looking up at the position of the stars.

His companions also consulted the great clock in the heavens. To be sure, they were late, the exercise had been somewhat prolonged.

Shambeje made a suggestion. 'The best thing for us to do is to complete the job tomorrow. We'll keep the corpse till then, agreed?'

And agree they all did. It would be better the following day; at least the job could be finished in a more relaxed fashion.

The following night, Kamukolo, whose spies had let him into this dark secret, managed to get into Shambeje's house and, in order to hide, he stretched out near to the body, which was wrapped in some material used for lining the roof. 'I also want to know who is the cleverer: you as a sorcerer, or me as a thief. At least, I knew what you were, but you don't know what I am... A sorcerer is a sorcerer, and a thief is a thief. Right, then! The sorcerer is acquainted with the world of evil, but, watch out, the thief knows all the tricks!' So he mused to himself, enjoying the prospects.

At dead of night, Shambeje gave the bundle a tug. But, instead of yielding, it rolled ponderously back into position.

'Hah! It doesn't want to come out! You'd think it actually likes being where it is!...' joked Shambeje.

His accomplices couldn't understand it. Why was it so heavy?

'When I give it a tug, the wretched thing rolls back again...' explained Shambeje, trying once again.

With a mocking laugh, his partner went round to the other end of the corpse. 'It won't resist any more this time! You get hold of the thing by the shoulders, and I'll get hold of the feet!'

And so, cursing and fuming, they managed to heave the body into the same litter it had been in the night before. Pleased with their efforts, off they set to the den where they were in the habit of performing their diabolical rituals...

Intent on going through with his scheme, Kamukolo clambered out of his hiding place, seized a magic amulet and set out in healthy pursuit. At a remote spot, in a dense thicket that had been transformed into a weird grotto, he was able to witness the macabre goings-on. Lashed to a framework of stakes, the body was already ablaze in the intense heat of the logs beneath it. Around it the sorcerers danced an infernal dance and had made themselves hideous to look upon. They waggled their feet about, their buttocks jerked and heaved, their voices chanted hoarsely as though they were goats, and then they took to whistling and screeching. Their appearance, made the more unearthly by the blaze from the fire, was such that they no longer seemed to be men but seemed genuinely to have become creatures from another world. On their heads, to suggest horns, they each wore a heron's plume, an *andua*'s plume[3] and a tuft of elephant hair. From their brows there hung, as a sort of mask, twigs and foliage, which permitted glimpses of the black and red streaks on their faces, as they swung to and fro. From their waists there hung down, like emblems, four more branches (one at the back, one at the front, and one on each flank), all rustling gleefully.

Seeking to share in the macabre feast, the tall flames licked at the corpse's flesh. Already it was crackling and emitting a smell of burning. Suddenly, Shambeje stopped and observed with a sarcastic leer: 'Just look at him! Isn't he nice and fat! And where did all his vanity get him in the end? Ho! Ho! Ho!'

'Where did it get him? It got him here, so we could eat him! Hah! What else could possibly have been his fate?' answered his partner mockingly.

Their companions, baring their teeth in satanic fashion, in their turn acted out their part in this sacrilegious performance. If other pompous men could only see the juicy steak that awaited the four of them, said one, they would have a greater sense of fear. To so many people the sorcerer was a person of little consequence. Well, such people were like dogs, they thought they were good people! Right there, in the blaze, such lofty airs just went up in smoke!...

---

[3] The *andua* (a Kimbundu word) is a bird native to Angola (*Caryathan livingstonia*), notable for its red plumage (TN).

These remarks seemed to crackle from their lips with the same glee as the crackling of the fire. In their excitement, these monsters started clapping their hands together in time with the rhythm of their macabre dancing.

'This was the scoundrel who tried to humiliate me,' called out Shambeje. 'Do you remember the time when we had the plague going round? I went along to try to borrow a bull from him, because mine had died from the disease, and my cows were in need of a bull. What answer do you suppose he gave me? "The plague hasn't reached the place where I live, as you very well know. If I lend you a bull, he might die, just like yours did. Surely your cows will find a male somewhere out there in the savanna." Much good his cattle are to him now!'

'Oh, come along, never mind all that. Let's get on with eating him, he smells good!' broke in one of his companions, cheerfully sniffing at the exciting aroma coming from the strange, strange roast.

Shambeje took a toasted cob of fermented manioc out of a kind of sack. 'All right, I'll use this cob to see what he tastes like,' he exclaimed. He soaked large lumps of manioc in the boiling fat and distributed them among his accomplices.

His partner chewed this appetizer with relish. Snarling angrily, he announced the name of another possible victim. 'Kamanga is another who needs this treatment. He's never done anything against me so far, but I'll provoke him into it, even if I have to go and chip away at his very door.'

Shambeje's reaction was cautious. 'Very well, he'll come here one day, and so will others. But not just yet. Let him pass for a while, otherwise people will start to get suspicious.'

A pack of howling prairie wolves went by, some way off.

'Keep away, keep away, this isn't for you,' guffawed one of the guests at the banquet.

The fourth one was quite confident that their den would frighten anything away. 'Of what use is our magic, if it can't keep them away?'

'Anyway, they're simply on the move, they live around here!' explained Shambeje's partner.

Meanwhile, the corpse had become nicely roasted and was crackling merrily, all smoke and bubbles. The aroma was now much stronger and was no longer confined to the den. It drifted forth, temptingly, capable of awakening cannibalistic urges. Kamukolo, who was still hiding in a thicket, was filled with horror and nausea, yet he persisted in watching the weird spectacle. So this was what sorcerers were like! In normal society they behaved decently, yet here they could be mistaken for wild beasts! Not just content with killing people, they ate them as well!

Intensifying their demoniac show, the sorcerers went on with their macabre prancing. With their convulsive jerking, they abandoned individual personality and once again resembled creatures of fantasy. And the roasted flesh went on explosively spitting and sputtering and crackling, letting out smoke and strange vapours.

'Shall we turn the lad over? He must be tired of being on his back!' suggested Shambeje, posting himself close to this revolting grill.

His companions thought it was a good idea. And so all of them, one here, another there, helped to turn the body over, grimacing ferociously as they did so. While it cooked on the other side, they greedily feasted on the part that was ready to eat.

'Aargh! It's like a nightmare! I trust no evil fate awaits me as a result of all this!' muttered Kamukolo, deeply shocked and alarmed, drawing away from the scene with the very same caution with which he had arrived.

'What can that be?' Shambeje wondered the following morning, noticing that Kamukolo was displaying a piece of red cloth on his person. In a swift series of sidelong glances, Shambeje examined it and felt his heart nearly stop. But Kamukolo just pretended he didn't notice and went on working alongside the other members of the chief's circle. Shambeje could control his anxiety no longer. He dashed home. Ah! It was *his* piece of cloth! The scoundrel! Not only that, he'd also stolen his precious sack of sorcerer's effects!

In a fury, he went back to the ceremonial tree. Kamukolo was still there, brazenly sporting the piece of cloth.

'Now I really do accept that the thief goes out before the sorcerer,' he rasped, tetchily.

No longer able to hide his excitement, the thief Kamukolo counter-attacked. 'Well, isn't that what I told you? At the time the thief is about, the sorcerer has still to go out!'

'But why is it always just you who answers me when I speak?' Objected Shambeje, with ill-disguised rage.

'Eh? Don't you remember?'

'Remember what?'

'Our bet...'

'The one you made the day before yesterday... And I'm the one who's won. Do you remember how the poor wretch wouldn't budge? Well, that was me yanking the other way...'

Shambeje saw his mistake in a flash. Now he could see the edge of the precipice to which his deeds had brought him. Though still trusting his supernatural powers, he could now feel the icy grip of fear. Forcing a smile yet cursing deep within himself, he cunningly sought to divert all suspicion. 'Aha! That's how I like people to be! One good joke deserves another!' Taking out his pipe, he asked, 'Have you got something there I can light this with?'

Those nearby, whose eyes were on their work but whose ears were following the conversation closely, were already muttering to one another in inquisitive undertones. What was all this really about? Was it serious or not? Certainly, in their midst, there was one who was a thief and one who was a sorcerer. But which was which? And what was the meaning of the piece of red cloth? No, this conversation was no mere joking matter. And anyway Shambeje did have his reputation of being a sorcerer!...

'I've nothing to light your pipe with! And anyway, I'm not joking, I saw everything, everything, everything! And don't pretend it wasn't you who wanted to place the bet!' retorted Kamukolo waspishly.

Shambeje didn't answer and was secretly trying to summon up the help of the spirit world. In his deep anxiety, he was trying everything to cause Kamukolo to drop dead there and then, as this was the only way he could escape the trouble he had so senselessly brought on himself. This scene was now followed by the chief, seated on his throne, who occasionally fanned himself with the tail of an antelope, and by his counsellors from their stools, who were silently carrying out their various tasks. What an extraordinary conversation, they thought. Thief and sorcerer, sorcerer and thief, they were still at it, even now! Perhaps it would be better to listen carefully, to make sure no villainy was afoot. But Kimone Kya Songa took a severe tone with the two and refused to contain his curiosity any longer. 'Now, look here. What's all this about? Are you joking or serious? I insist on knowing.'

At this point, therefore, Kamukolo, to the astonishment of all present, related the macabre scene he had spied on.

'Eeeh! Sorcerer! So now we know who dug up Kifuba's body the day before yesterday!' shouted out the listeners, clapping their hand across their mouths.

Amid the ensuing hubbub, a number of them gathered round Kamukolo and, half in terror, half in admiration, sought to give him advice. He should be very careful now and should especially seek the services of a medicine man. Anybody who saw the sorcerer's den, that accursed place where they roasted dead bodies, must surely be in need of treatment. Nevertheless, what courage he had shown in witnessing such a spectacle!

'Ah, Kamukolo, how did your heart stand up to it? Didn't you tremble all over and go cold with fear?' asked Mukaluka, gaping at him, wide-eyed.

'Not a bit. Or at least, to begin with, I shuddered all over...'

'What a fine man you are!'

Kamukolo, warming to his account, now started imitating the sorcerer's antics, prancing about and squealing like a goat.

Guffaws and great hoots of laughter rent the air. What a rogue that Kamukolo was!

Meanwhile, Shambeje, who had already been tied up, was awaiting his accomplices, who were being rounded up by the tribal guards.

'I suppose you know what's in store for you and your gang?' the chief inquired of him sarcastically, coming forth from his palace with all his family retinue, whom he had called forth specially for the occasion.

Defeated, yet, deep within him, still trying to summon forth the protection of the spirits, Shambeje rolled his eyes upwards in hideous fashion.

'Ha! Just look at him, he's just like an owl!' guffawed one woman.

Others clapped their hands together, taunting him: 'Ooh! Just see the sorcerer's face!'

'What the Devil conceals, God reveals,' declared one of the counsellors ponderously.

Like a swarm of bees, the remarks buzzed about in the bright heat of advancing day. So these were the sorcerers who were making off with people from the village. Who could possibly have guessed what had been going on in their hearts? Yes, it really was quite true: what the Devil concealed, God revealed.

And as custom decreed, the four sorcerers hanged themselves by their own hands.

NIGHT OF NOSTALGIA

That Christmas Eve, Francisco Rebelo, who for many years had farmed in the Gumbe area, broke with the apathy of previous years and, more out of nostalgia than tradition, decided to celebrate Christmas night on his little ranch. In order to prevent the evening meal from becoming dull and monotonous, he had invited along the district officer and a trader, together with their families. If everybody's goodwill and joy were shared with everybody else, then the evening would be spent very happily. Once gathered together and all united by the same ideal, they could more fittingly relive life as it was led in their far-off home country.

While the customary chicken broth was being prepared in the kitchen, together with the inevitable dried cod and other delicacies, Francisco Rebelo turned on an old gramophone in his modest sitting room. With the music, the conversation died down, and a tender yearning enfolded the three men.

'The *fado*! Marvellous! It really gets to your heart!' sighed the trader as the last note of the record died away.

Francisco put another record on. 'Well, it's our national song, isn't it?'

'Of course it is. It's our national song and it's so plaintive. Its notes seem to express all the sentimentality of the Portuguese,' agreed the district officer.

'That's true. Each and every one of us surely heaves a great sigh whenever he thinks of life back home in Portugal,' added the trader.

'You're right,' said the district officer. 'I dare say we all go a bit wistful at the thought of the town or village we come from, when we think about the family we've left behind and all the good memories. Take today, for example. Today really fills me with nostalgia! I just remember how, at Christmas, all the family, my parents, my brothers and sisters and other members of the family as well..., how we all used to get together in a great family circle around the table. D'you know, the two old folks, surrounded by their children and their grandchildren, they were just like two trees, trees that, having lost all their leaves in winter, suddenly put out fresh spring shoots. As for us kids, well..., we didn't really appreciate just how moving an occasion it can be. All *we* could think about was that little Christmas tree... it was just a branch off a pine tree...there it was with all the presents on it! I can remember, I once wanted to have a drum. I really wanted to be a soldier and march up and down, banging it, like soldiers do. Till the moment when the birth of Baby Jesus was announced, which was when the presents were handed out, I made up for it by drumming on the chairs with my fingers. As for my grandmother, dear old thing, she just sat there, beaming with pleasure at seeing how happy we all were. Her smile must have been some sort of reflection of her own childhood. When she was a little girl she must have played like some butterfly sucking nectar from flowers. Not the flowers that grow in gardens, but other, sweeter, more delicate flowers... the flowers of innocence. Ah, well... Look just how quickly time passes us all by! Anyway, what is life but a pleasant puff on a cigarette!'

'Well said. Just a pleasant puff on a cigarette. That's because both burn away, both disappear, and all they leave behind is a pungent taste, a sort of acrid smell... in a word, just wistfulness,' added the trader.

Francisco downed what was left of his glass of port, and his two guests followed suit. He carried on with the discussion: 'Yes, it's when you're away from the place you come from, a long way from your family, that you start to get homesick for Portugal.'

The alcoholic vapours and the heady sound of further records now made him warm to his theme, to the point where patriotism overflowed. 'One's homeland... What an eloquent, sublime word it is, a word celebrated down the ages in prose and verse. It's only got eight letters, yet within its embrace lies all the territory of a whole people. If we're willing to sacrifice everything for our country... life, family, possessions... then, when so far away from her, how could we do anything other than experience an indefinable longing? If our home country is the mother of a whole people, how, then, could we do anything else but weep for her in our nostalgia? Since it is the cradle that rocked us the first time we cried, since it's the field where we sang and played and laughed, since it's that holy ground where our mortal remains may well come to rest, how could we do otherwise than keep a place for her in our hearts? She lulled us to sleep with sweet music, listened to us stammering our first words, and it was she and she alone who first showed us the diamonds that glitter in the night sky. Tears, sighs, moans, whatever it was, she consoled us. A true mother! In our upbringing and at school, in joy and in suffering, she did nothing but shower benefits on us. What better place could any of us live in than our homeland? What better place is there than home? Who better to look after us than our own mother? And what finer mother than our homeland, our mother-country? Ah, but man, always chasing after some new triumph..., he leaves home and family behind and goes off to distant lands. He gazes on little-known vistas, he admires monuments, he looks in amazement at grandiose palaces and so very easily forgets. He toils, he exhausts himself, he makes his pile. But, when ambition has grown weary, his mind carries him back to the little spot where he was born. And then, as he ponders, a sadness sweeps over him. What wouldn't he give now to be able to hug his parents once more! How he'd like to feel their warmth again, the warmth perhaps of two old, old people, their hair as white as snow, their cheeks hollowed out by life's storms, their eyes shadowed by the going down of the sun, and their bodies bent under the weight of years! Oh, and what about his childhood friends? Had they weathered the storm? Could they have done some deal with Mammon? Ah, how time flies! How many years must it be now? And then, as if by magic, this exiled man sees the church where he was baptized, the humble school where he first learned to read and write, where he first drank at the fount to which he has so often returned to quench his thirst. And so, one by one, the pearls of the past drop off the string... the happy times when he really enjoyed himself, the regional cooking that he so often enjoyed, the trees that provided the awning for the sweet joys of love's first awakening. All this, my friends, reaches deep into his heart. Plucking at its very strings, it converts the yearning, the longing, into sighs without number.'

Francisco's voice took on a sombre note as though he were making a confession. 'It's thirty-two years since I left Portugal. Since then, I've beavered away in this wretched land of fire, sometimes having to put up with this hot-headed local population, sometimes suffering from the destruction brought by locusts, and just occasionally making a profit when fortune has seen fit to smile on me. In a word, I'm just a cork, a cork tossed about on the ocean of life.'

'Well, frankly, in my case, I've endured twenty years out here,' declared the district officer.

The trader had no choice but to comment on his own situation: 'I've been here for fifteen. And all because of a woman!'

Francisco laughed. 'She didn't feel the same about you, I take it?'

'Oh, it was rather worse than that. I was cruelly, brutally let down. I could so easily have killed myself!'

'Good God!' exclaimed the district officer, in a tone of obvious irony. 'To look at you, you're perfectly cast for that kind of part!'

'Part! There's no play-acting in my case, just life itself, blast it! And we're all given ridiculous paths to follow, along the way. Sometimes, when we look back at our past lives, all we experience is shame. It's as though someone were mocking us.'

His two friends both smiled, not by way of disapproval, but because, deep down, they were in full agreement. Indeed, it was true that the present often made the past seem ridiculous. While they mused on this, the trader went on with his narrative.

'Whenever I think about that stupid incident, I could kick myself. It all happened in Lisbon. Just as any man might, I fell madly in love with this little blonde. She was a little darling, honestly. I really got carried away, I can tell you. We went out together for a while, until, suddenly, one day, just like a bucket of cold water poured over me, I got a letter from her calling it all off. It seemed she'd found some other lover boy whom she preferred to me! I was completely stunned by the whole thing, then offended, then furious. I got so desperate, all I wanted to do was die. Life no longer meant anything any more. I just lay on my wretched bed with my head buried in the pillows and wept. I took to thinking about the easiest way I could do away with myself. Yes, I'd hang myself. But then, in my mind's eye, I could picture how I would look: my face like a mask, my eyes fixed in a horrible stare, my tongue sticking out. Oof, no! I found the idea quite terrifying. So I changed my plan; I would cut my carotid arteries. That way, I wouldn't look so ghastly when dead. But, on second thoughts, it occurred to me that committing suicide in that fashion would put me on the same level as pigs. So, with my eyes full of tears, I finally opted for poison. Once I'd bought the poison, I set off on a tram bound for the zoo.'

Francisco Rebelo and the district officer were now quietly and intently listening to this account with faint smiles playing around their lips. The trader just carried on.

'As the tram went from street to street, people got on and got off and went past me in complete indifference to me. I felt as though everything around me was dead. I can still even remember a street urchin who jumped onto the tram as nimbly as a monkey and yelled in my ear: *'Faithful*! Get your copy of *Old Faithful*! It's belly laughs from cover to cover! Go on, buy one!' I just shoved him away. I can still hear him shouting something about me being a lousy bastard. Meanwhile, the tram jolted onwards, stopping and starting, putting people down and picking people up, till suddenly there I was at the zoo. I sat on a bench in a quiet shady corner and smoked a cigarette, then another and another till I lost count. Without really wanting to, I found myself letting my mind wander away from all my troubles. As if by some miracle brought on by nostalgia, I started picturing myself as a boy playing bows and arrows, dressed in shorts down to my knees, my hair all windswept and my cheeks all flushed from rushing about. I found myself recalling various stages of my life till finally there I was, back at the door of this damn girl. Then, when I remembered how she'd been kissed by this other character, I was seized by a mixture of anger and dismay. In blind jealousy, dammit, I raised the bottle to my lips. Then, and this is the extraordinary part, it's as if some secret voice spoke to me, so that my arm just fell to my side again, and I burst into tears. They were really hot tears, as though they weren't just coming from my eyes but from the very depths of my soul. Mysteriously, I was now full of remorse and could now picture my parents' home. I could see my father weeping and my mother wailing disconsolately. I read the accounts of my own tragic end in the newspapers. But once again my insane jealousy for this wretched girl took a stronger hold, and so yet again I lifted the bottle to my mouth. Nonetheless, the invisible force brought my hand back down again. "Just what are you going to do?" I heard myself say in a tone of reproach. Bewildered and frightened, I asked out loud: "Shall I drink it or shall I not?" Once more, like flashes of lightning at night in a thunderstorm, there, dancing before my eyes, was my boyhood, my adolescence, my family. Only then did I recognize how stupidly wrong I was. In a panic, I smashed the bottle and virtually ran away from the place, muttering to myself: "No, good grief, no. You've only got one life, and the world's full of women!" So, shortly afterwards, I made up my mind to go to Africa, where I could make money more easily. That way, I'd be able one day to walk past that damn woman and just look at her with contempt.'

Then, with an ironic tone in his voice, he summed it all up: 'That's my little love drama, then.'

'Well, when we're young, we get up to strange things,' admitted the district officer.

'Yes, but even so, I'd give a lot to be that age again,' cut in Francisco, with obvious regret.

'Quite so, I agree with you,' agreed the district officer.

They fell silent. From the servants' compound there echoed the noise of dancing and festivities.

'Hah! Even the blacks are celebrating Christmas,' joked the trader, more to break the silence, than out of a desire to seem witty.

Francisco nodded sympathetic agreement. 'Ah, yes, poor people, although they've no idea of the importance of this particular day, they've got a perfect right to enjoy themselves too. After all, they are our workforce.'

The district officer took this up. 'You know, I've noticed something about these people, that even when they're enjoying themselves, their singing has a rather plaintive ring to it.'

'Yes, I've thought a lot about that, too. It really is quite true, it seems to me, that there's something mournful about their songs, something that reaches out and strikes a tender and nostalgic chord in us too. Apparently, according to some authorities on the subject, the black race had at one time reached a high level of civilization.[1] You don't suppose that this plaintiveness is the reflection of some deep nostalgia?'

'Well, perhaps'

'And anyway, why not? Quite possibly the loss of such a civilization produced such intense anguish that it stretched the feelings of their forebears to the absolute limits, and then, subsequently, in some form of ancestor worship, has come to be passed down from generation to generation. And so now, in an involuntary, unwitting fashion, they're lamenting their misfortune.'

'Your argument, my dear Rebelo, is really very interesting. It wouldn't surprise me at all if that were the case, especially if one takes into account some of the odd features of telegony. At any rate, my own view is that the most reasonable explanation is that Nature, with her own skilful way of arranging things, has filled them with sadness, so that their feelings should correspond to the colour of mourning represented in their skin.'

---

[1] 'The hereditary literature of the black peoples, which is capable of rivalling that of any race, provides yet one more piece of evidence that the black man is not some being fated to be inferior, as many people still claim, either out of prejudice or out of superficial acquaintance.' So wrote the Swiss scholar Héli Châtelain in 1888 (Author's Note – AN).

A group of children barged into the room, interrupting the conversation and excitedly announcing that the chicken broth was already on the table.

The trader chuckled. 'I think there's a lot that's right in what you both say. But the rightest thing of all just now is to do justice to the meal...'

The tom-tom went on beating. Amid the greatest enjoyment, wild tribal songs echoed from over a hundred pairs of lungs and mingled with high-pitched whistling. Stimulated by the frenzied rhythm, men and women joined in the dancing and whirled about in their excitement. By now, the maize wine and the cane spirit had passed from gourds to stomachs, and the vapours therefrom were causing their uncivilized brains to reel. As night advanced, the alcohol intensified their merrymaking, as they laughed and sang and danced. Suddenly, there came a halt to their enthusiasm. What was it? A case of infidelity. Swiftly, people took sides.

'If that rascal knew that the woman had already got her own man, then why did he persist in speaking to her? Isn't that just taking a liberty and treating people with contempt? After all, if he didn't talk to her, she wouldn't go running after him. So he's a scoundrel, and they both deserve a good thrashing,' accused the supporters of the man who had been the victim of the infidelity.

'It's hardly his fault; it's the woman who's a good-for-nothing. What did she accept for? Hadn't she already got her own man? Is she a child, to be so easily led?' So ran the argument of those who supported the man responsible.

The debate raged until the elders finally reached their decision. As the maize harvest had not yet begun, then the couple should remain together until the appropriate time, so that, afterwards, they could make due division of their produce.

So the festivities began again, till their enthusiasm resounded far into the distance. The jungle, adding its own great chorus, warmly intoned a lullaby to the holiness of Christmas night.

'Silva, I'm not sure if you're aware whom we have to thank for this delightful evening,' said the district officer as he tackled a leg of roast turkey.

With a roguish smile, the trader blandly replied: 'Well, who d'you think? Old Rebelo here, with his brilliant idea of inviting us to share supper with him...'

Little chuckles broke out among the wives and children.

'It's certainly no "cardinals' supper"...,'[2] declared Francisco Rebelo, pouring out glasses of frothing *vinho verde*.[3]

With his well-filled glass already half the way to his lips, the trader quipped in the same tone: 'Hah! That's the title of a play by Júlio Dantas! Out here in Africa we'll have to call it "the settlers' supper"!'

'Well said, Mr Silva, well said!' called out the lady of the house, clapping her hands together in pleasure at how well the party was going.

'Right, then, so we'll call it "the settlers' supper",' agreed the district officer, 'but who do we have to thank for it?'

'Have a bit of wing, Mr Silva?' asked Mrs Rebelo invitingly.

'Yes, please, certainly. If I've got to deal with a turkey-hen, then I'd better get a good dose of turkey-cock first,' joked Silva, with a chuckle. Then, turning to the district officer, he went on: 'Go on, tuck in, Antunes; at any rate, you don't have to thank me for it.'

---

[2] A reference to the celebrated one-act play *A Ceia dos Cardeais* (1902), by the Portuguese dramatist Júlio Dantas (TN).

[3] Literally, 'green wine', a young Portuguese semi-sparkling wine. 'Green' refers to the wine's youth, not its colour. Both red and white varieties are to be found (TN).

'Don't take any notice of what my husband says, Mr Antunes,' interjected the trader's wife. 'Just say what you were going to say. He's already had one over the eight.'

Silva let out a guffaw: 'Only if it's on your watch!... According to mine,' he said, peering at it, 'it's five minutes to one...'

'Fine! As you wish, then, so you've had one over the five!' joked the district officer. Then, becoming serious again amid the general hilarity, he added: 'The answer is, my dear Mrs Silva, that we owe this supper to the hunger of the ancient Christians.'

'Oh, now really, Antunes, come on! Surely this supper is something we owe to the good-heartedness of Rebelo here?'

'Just be quiet, for Heaven's sake!' said his wife crossly. 'Do go on, Mr Antunes.'

'That's right, you tick him off. Well, now, it seems that on this date, because their faith was a lot stronger in those days, they all used to fast from noon till midnight. And then, when they got back from Midnight Mass, they used to eat something to assuage their hunger. And so, what began as a necessity, bit by bit down the centuries has become transformed into a delightful social and festive occasion. Not only that, but to heighten the event still further, there came about the practice of giving and receiving special presents on this day as well.'

'For me, Christmas Day is the most beautiful day of the year,' declared Francisco Rebelo, as though making a great speech.

Similar appreciative comments followed. Yes, Christmas commemorated a most cherished event. Rich and poor, young and old, everybody celebrated this particular day. Often travelling from far and wide, children would return home for that day to visit their parents, to restore the links in the chain broken by the demands of human existence.

Shining brightly, and forever gently hissing, the oil lamp in its niche seemed to share the joy around the table. In the distance could be heard the friendly rhythm of the dancers, while within the house the gentle aroma of sweetmeats drifted over the diners, filling them with a delightful, voluptuous sense of satisfaction and well-being. There were doughnuts, pancakes, rice pudding, raisins, figs and roast chestnuts, all washed down with port, brandy and champagne. Over all this reigned the increasing good humour of everybody present.

'Now that I've started, I'm going to finish my little lesson, provided nobody objects,' announced the district officer in an even more jovial mood. 'You see, in days of yore, today wasn't today.'

'Really? So today wasn't today?' queried Mrs Rebelo, busily passing sweets and special Christmas buns around the children.

Perched on the roof was some bird noisily uttering its treacherous call that echoed harshly through the night air: '*Hosi, hosi, o manu a kasi kulo.*' ('Lion, lion, there are people here.')

Enlivened by the alcohol, the trader, whose voice now rose higher than everybody else's (which amused the servants), attempted a humorous answer: 'No, Ana, in days of yore, today *was* today! That's right, isn't it, Antunes? Eh? Come on now, eh?'

More because of his silly laugh than his wit, everybody was infected by his hilarity and burst out laughing.

'Just listen to the scoundrel!' chuckled the district officer.

'You've really had one too many this time!' said Francisco Rebelo, grinning broadly. Quietly, he made the decision to repeat the party the following year.

Standing behind his master, his servant meekly but enviously reflected on the spread that the guests had demolished. 'Master, us not get a Chrissima?' he asked, plucking up courage in view of the general mood of benevolence.

Francisco Rebelo felt a sudden surge of generosity. Getting up from the table, he personally went over to the sideboard, opened it and took out a bottle of port and a selection of candied sweets. 'These are for you all to share among you, all right?'

'Francisco, just a minute, I've got something for them as well,' broke in his wife, as she too got up from the table.

Outside, the orchard cast its spell: crooawk... crooawk... crooawk..., as the frogs, harbingers of the approaching rain, joined together in a monotonous symphony.

'But, as you were saying, Mr Antunes,' recalled the trader's wife, 'hasn't Christmas always fallen on December 25th?'

Taking a long pull on his cigar, the district officer replied: 'No, madam. In former times, in the first two centuries of the Christian era, that's to say, up to about the year 200, the birth of Jesus was sometimes celebrated in January and sometimes in May.'

Mrs Silva let out a gasp of surprise. 'Is that so? D'you mean that, at that time, people didn't know when Christ was born?'

'You never told me anything about this!' complained the district officer's wife.

'That was simply because the occasion never arose.' Turning to Mrs Silva, he went on: 'You see, the fact is that those who celebrated Christmas like that certainly didn't know the exact date. So much so, that Bishop Cystus of Jerusalem asked Pope Julius I to seek out the opinions of eminent theologians, of men who studied religion closely. And, as a result, Christmas Day was finally fixed on December 25th.'

'Poor Baby Jesus, not having a definite birthday!' whined the trader's wife, before suddenly switching her mood to one of delight, 'Oh, look, a white butterfly!'

Mrs Rebelo chimed in: 'That's a clear sign of good news!'

'At this time especially, it must be a bearer of good wishes from friends and relatives far away!' added Mrs Silva, with increasing zest.

'If that's the case,' boomed Silva, 'let's drink a toast to their health.'

The champagne glasses were primed. Everybody drank an effusive toast to absent friends.

'To the prosperity of Portugal!' proposed the district officer.

Once more the glasses clinked together.

'Aren't you forgetting my country?' protested Mrs Rebelo playfully. Within her veins flowed the blood of an inter-racial alliance between Portugal and Angola.

'My wife's quite right,' declared Francisco Rebelo. 'If Angola is in our debt for her spiritual progress, we're in her debt for our material progress. Let's all drink a toast to Angola. To Angola, everybody!'

Meanwhile, the rhythmic dancing went on throbbing away down in the village, harshly, continuously: ta-ta-tum..., ta-ta-tum..., ta-ta-tum...

HEBO

Hebo sat at the door of her house, captivated by the magic of the afternoon, fondly daydreaming about her own future chances in life. She could already picture herself as the wife of some wealthy and slenderly-built gentleman, living in style, with lots of servants to do all the work for her. In her conceited way, she felt that this agreeable status would be due reward for her considerable beauty.

She had, after all, been courted by men of no little standing. But none had been able to capture her affections. For all their expensive presents, she had remained aloof and turned them all away. Their surprised reaction was to wonder whether Hebo was in some way incapable of love. But no: not all keys can unlock the same door.

Hebo was still enjoying this pleasurable glow, when she was approached by a stranger who was bent on putting to the test the stories that were told about how conceited she was. He asked for a piece of wood from the fire so that he could light his pipe. Hebo took one look at his shabby appearance and sneered: 'What? Are you crazy? Do you think I'm going to get up to give you a light?'

'Aha! Do you mean to say that to get up to give me a light is beneath your dignity?' the man retorted.

72

'Oh, go away! Don't come looking for trouble with me! I wouldn't stoop to your superiors, let alone you. You stink like a stray cat! Go on, get away from me and don't give me your insolence!'

The stranger went away. Yet, in the very midst of his humiliation, he was planning just how he was going to get his revenge. He had quite naturally expected her to refuse, but not to be abusive as well. The thing to do, therefore, was to go and seek out a witchdoctor, so that her sneers and ill manners could be turned against her. For this plan to bear fruit, he had to walk for many, many miles, suffering the oppressive heat of several days' journey. At last he spoke to the witchdoctor.

'I want that woman to be mine, but without declaring myself to her. So I don't want *kilemba* or *dishikane* [1] or anything like that...'

Having gone through the appropriate ritual, he then listened as the witchdoctor intoned the secret spell and concluded with the following command: 'Change yourself into a bird and snatch the girl away with your mighty talons.'

In a sudden transformation, the vengeful stranger slowly and ponderously rose up into the air. Flapping his huge wings he flew away, intermittently cawing: 'Here I come... Here I come... Here I come to get my revenge.'

People took fright when they saw the enormous bird and heard its strange cry. What was the meaning of the strange apparition? What portent did it bear? Dear God, what could it be?

'Keep well away from us, dread omen!' they chanted, forming a cross with their forefingers in an attempt to exorcise it.

But the winged figure, immune to all exorcism, flew steadily on.

'Here I come... Here I come... Here I come to get my revenge.'

---

[1] *Kilemba* or *dishikane* (Kimbundu words) are preparations of certain powdered leaves which, when eaten or rubbed on the body, were thought greatly to assist hitherto disappointed suitors (TN).

It was night when he arrived at Hebo's village. Alighting on a tree near her house, he broke the nocturnal silence with this chant:

Here I am, lovely Hebo,
here I am to take you away.
Arise and come with me.

The girl woke up and shuddered with fright. What had she heard? Could it have been a dream? But the bird soon began its sinister chant once more:

Here I am, lovely Hebo,
here I am to take you away.
Arise and come with me.

Fear welled up in her throat as though to form a scream. But the sound would not come. Desperately she tried to run. But the muscles of her legs would not respond.

With increasing menace the bird now called out again:

Don't you hear my voice?
Hurry up, or I'll throttle you!

Breaking free from the bonds of panic, Hebo got up. But she was not yet free from her bemused state and mechanically packed a bundle of belongings in readiness to leave, just as a simple-minded person, hypnotized by the gaze of a snake, is drawn inexorably towards its jaws. Suddenly she awoke from her mental torpor. She ran to her parents' room. Weeping aloud, she shook them violently: 'Father, mother, wake up, a bird has come to take me away!'

But her parents did not hear. They were both in a deep, deep sleep, a sleep that – horror of horrors – seemed like the sleep of death.

With the same baleful tone the bird's chant rang out again:

Don't you hear my voice?
Hurry up, or I'll throttle you!

Overcome with anguish, Hebo scrambled her way to the alcove where her brothers slept and sought their protection, beside herself with terror: 'Brothers, wake up, wake up, I'm going to be killed!'

But her brothers did not hear. They too were all in a deep, deep sleep, a sleep that – alas! – again seemed like the sleep of death.

Outside the bird grimly flapped its wings. Poor girl, she was utterly helpless! With one last desperate effort Hebo cried out: 'Neighbours, neighbours, come and save me, a bird has come to take me away!'

But the neighbours did not come. Like her parents and her brothers, they were all in a deep, deep sleep, a sleep that – oh, spirits of the next world – seemed like the sleep of death.

With an extraordinary beating of wings the bird flew onto the house, made a hole in the thatched roof and snatched away the poor girl.

Next morning the household was filled with horror. The roof had a great hole in it! Hebo was nowhere to be found! What could have happened?

Their cries attracted the neighbours, the whole house became a very tempest of questions and answers. Amid the storm of speculation, an old woman, like the sun breaking through the mist, repeated the terrible chanting she had heard the night before. She had not summoned anybody: she had been too petrified with fright.

'Because of her haughty manner a magician has stolen her away!' That was the conclusion they all came to.

Dawn was breaking when the bird made its descent to a certain township. Still in a state of bewilderment, Hebo beheld the bird take on human form. She stood there stupefied as she recognized the man she had treated so badly.

'Do you know who I am?' he asked, with a huge guffaw.

'Aaah! Don't kill me! Please forgive me!'

'Are you trembling? Are you afraid of the man who smells like a stray cat? There's no need to be afraid, I'm not going to kill you. The stray cat only eats chickens, he doesn't eat people...'

'Please forgive me, sir! You're quite right!'

'Huh! Just look at that face! So full of conceit. Well, let me tell you something: I'm the man with whom you're going to set up house,' and he beat his chest with his fist. 'Yes, me, the man who smells like a stray cat! D'you hear? That's just to get rid of your insolence!'

Years later, the former huge bird, now the father of three sons, introduced himself, along with his wife and children, to Hebo's family. He told them the story of his revenge and presented them with the traditional bride-price.

And as the reward for her arrogance, Hebo now wore the crown of humility.

(Folktale)

THE TENDER MIAOW

Standing on a verdant spot, out in the Bié area, was a small trading store, with its farmyard to one side, while on the other stood the house of adobe walls, in front of which there stretched a garden, well stocked with vegetables and fruit trees. Here they both worked, bound together by their love of the soil and for each other, vigorously bending their backs in a common cause. For some years now they had lived together: he was a Portuguese settler; his common-law wife was a daughter of the Angolan savanna.

Like the hot, life-giving rays of the sun, he had brought from his native land a burning faith in his ability to succeed, a faith that was locked deep within his heart. Wearing the youthful armour of his twenty-four years, he had had all the impetuous zeal he needed to do battle with Africa. Had he no fear? No, none at all, death doesn't choose any particular places. One day, therefore, like the flower that mellows into fruit, he would see all his sacrifices transformed: a dazzling triumph would be his reward.

He had begun his venturesome crusade by working first here, then there, then somewhere else, often undergoing bitter experiences.

'Is it much further now, boy?' he kept asking the bearers on that occasion, long ago, in Zaire province, as they made their way to a trading post to which he had been recommended for a job.

As they were all good walkers with little regard for distances, the bearers cheerfully answered: 'No, master. Jus' a bit mo'; jus' over there,' pointing towards a hill.

The sun beat down. From the seashore rose up soft suffocating vapours. Further away, aggressive but useless, stood clumps of thorn bushes and occasional baobab trees, while beyond, even more mercilessly, there stretched away areas that were totally barren. Aided only by the sand beneath his feet and the coolness of the spray, he trudged along the shore all afternoon. His only thought was to arrive, to reach his goal as quickly as possible. He was consoled by the bearers' assurance.

'Boy, is it much further on? We're well past the hill...,' he eventually complained.

His servants, who were interested only in the direction, not in the location, simply pointed ahead again, not at the next hill (as it appeared to him), but simply at what stretched out before them: 'No, master. Jus' a bit mo'; jus' over there...'

Only finally, after many hours' journey, with his feet covered in blisters, did he reach his objective. Exhaustion had made him give in to feelings of regret and despondency, but now that he had at last reached his destination, hope rose again in his heart.

Later, borne along by ambition, he got himself dispatched to Catumbela, which was then a thriving market for exports. There, in that busy market, he took part in belly-dancing and sang in chorus with pretty black girls.

'Now the fire dance!' the master of ceremonies would order.

Everybody would clap hands in unison, and the noise would resound throughout the vast hall, bedecked with palm fronds.

'Take your partners!'

To the rhythm of the harmonica and the rattle-gourd, the couples minced round in a great circle. Occasionally, a European dancer would call out in his enthusiasm.

Later on still, in his anxiety to forge ahead, he had settled in Bié, though now quite independently, as the owner of a small ranch. There, more out of convenience than for any physical reason, he decided to live with his woman, this daughter of the savanna. Little by little, as though allowing her to share in the glow that blazed within him, he opened up small areas of civilization to her, casting her in new moulds, as he saw fit. From that wild tree he received not only the shade of the help he had taught her to give him, but also those fruits that he had sweetened with his love: his children.

His days were spent in the endless toil of trade. In steady droves, men and women arrived carrying rubber or wax. The men's scalps were shaven at the sides, leaving only a central tuft or plume, and on each wrist they wore two or three hoops. The women's hair was worn in tresses greased with castor oil or tacula oil and adorned with little coloured beads; at the end of the tresses they wore an extra large bead or a sea-shell, while on their heads, like a diadem, was a whole swathe of tiny beads; half way along their forearms they wore two broader beads on each arm and the same on each ankle, as well as metal bracelets; their teeth had an angled gap cut between the central upper incisors, in contrast to those of the Ganguela people who sharpen them; on their forehead and temples stood out tattoo markings cut with a small, sharp knife; the marks respectively depicted three stripes and what looked like a small key; through their ear lobes they wore a sliver of wood that was thicker at the front. Both sexes covered themselves with a loincloth that hung down from the waist to the knees, the men winding the cloth around twice, whilst, to protect their breasts, the women wore a strip of cloth wrapped around diagonally.

'Good day, Katemo, I've come for gunpowder and striped chintz,' demanded some great native merchant, arriving on his cart with a whole caravan of bearers behind him. The shop was a hubbub of voices and seemed like a hive. Some people bartered, whilst others just gossiped. Frequent outbreaks of loud laughter bore witness to the good humour of these simple people. Everywhere seemed to be permeated with the smell of bodies. But our trader didn't hear the noise nor smell the stench: his sole concern was to do business.

'Right you are, sir! Here's the gunpowder..., and here's your chintz cloth. Is there anything else I can get for you?' he said, beaming at the big shot.

The merchant joked: 'Oh, all sorts of things... Your shop could never have all I want.'

'We'll soon see about that. Tell me, my friend,' he said, slapping his customer on the back, 'what else do you want?'

'Very well. Can you let me have some spirits and tobacco?'

The trader bustled about in the limited space available, filling gourds with spirits distilled from the sweet potato and placing dry tobacco leaves in layers in baskets.

Outside, there was plenty of activity taking place. Sitting on the grass, under orange trees and lemon trees, or even standing, some people were lazily chewing roast sweet potato or roast corn cobs; others were absorbedly pounding away on marimbas; yet others were puffing their pipes and chattering with excited gestures.

'Oh yes, Katemo, I'll be needing some pipes and some tin tacks,' added his wealthy customer jauntily, just as Katemo was packing everything up.

Our trader's enthusiasm grew at the excellent business he was doing.

'Just as you say. You can have everything I've got if you like.'

Some of the bystanders pretended to protest. 'Everything? And what about us? Isn't our rubber as good as his? Don't give him anything else.'

Still measuring out, the trader retorted: 'If things run out, I'll work a spell, and the shop will be back to normal.'

'Ha! Fibber! Who on earth ever taught you how to work a spell?' they scoffed.

Meanwhile, the customer placed another order: 'Katemo, let me have some beads and some salt as well.'

Finally, the trader inquired: 'What's all this for? To set you up with even more women?'

'Women? It's to help me with my business! I'm off to Ganguelas to buy slaves.' As the trader just stood there looking at him in silence, he went on: 'Right then, what are you going to give me for free, by way of a discount?... After all, look at all I've bought...'

Jerked out of the sudden shock produced by the appalling admission, the trader beat his forehead: 'Of course, of course, sorry! What would you like?'

His customer, who, unlike the others, dressed in European style, pondered hesitantly: 'Let me see now..., I'd like a..., I know, I'd like some boots, a hat and a shirt.'

The trader whistled in surprise: 'That's rather a lot! Can't you reduce it a bit?'

'A lot? After all I've bought?'

'Yes, but... How about just the footwear?'

'Oh, all right, then. Just the boots. And a glass of spirits as well...'

Finally, off he went with his retinue. Because of wild animals, all his servants had small bells fastened to their belts, and these jingled as they headed away.

The next person to be served was a woman. She also jingled as she walked, but the bells were inside her dress, simply to reveal that she was pregnant. She was accompanied by an old man. Owing to his age, his head was completely bald.

The trader happily busied himself with his customers, exchanging jokes with everybody, which he was well able to do, as he spoke their language fluently, and went on heaping up the rubber and the ivory that they brought him. These two products were their chief means of trading, other than the slave trade. Later, to a chorus of loud songs and rhythmic chanting, a jingling band of blacks would set off for Benguela or Catumbela, transporting the loads of rubber and ivory on a journey that would take several days, weeks, even a month and a half. Moreover, the route, by virtue of the frequent attacks to which they might be subjected, followed a line worked out on the basis of the protection afforded by alliances. Such alliances made by their own chief with other chiefs in the areas they had to pass through. Quite apart from the danger of having their merchandise plundered, there was the additional risk of being sold into slavery, from which a man could only escape if his family paid a large ransom.

Sometimes he had to act as a sort of judge.

'Katemo,' they would urge, 'we've come to get your verdict.'

'Oh? Why, what's the dispute about?'

Then those in dispute would all talk and wave their arms about and give their reasons for this and that, while he sat there listening patiently, because he was well acquainted with their customs.

'White man, if this fellow has been with my girl, he must pay an indemnity. I want a pig from him.'

'Us whites, when a woman misbehaves herself, what we do is send her away. Why don't you send her packing?'

'But that's the white man's way!... D'you think I'm going to give her up, just so that he'll be able to have a good laugh at my expense? No, Katemo, I need to teach him a lesson, or he'll poke fun...'

And so, the settler, promoted to the role of judge because of his quick wits, found himself frequently settling disputes in accordance with customary tribal law. To go against this would be to do violence to a collective consciousness moulded by thousands of years.

In spite of all this activity, however, from time to time he was beset by the loneliness of his existence. But, thanks to the promptings of ambition, his business prospered. They called him Katemo, which means 'Spade', this being a picturesque epithet deriving from his great devotion to his small-holding: vegetables, potatoes, sweet potatoes, corn, maize, beans, oranges, lemons. What European, up country, didn't have some nickname? Not one. After all, it was so often a sign of popularity, rather than of ridicule.

Eventually, the settler began to yearn to revisit the place of his birth. He would take his children with him on the journey, they'd learn a lot from it. But fate, which is as capricious as time, swiftly stepped in.

'Katemo, we're going to have to run for it! The local chieftain, you know, Dumduma, he's threatening to kill all the whites!' So said the woman with whom he lived, one day back in 1902.

He was sitting making some notes in his modest sitting room at the time. He looked at her and just laughed. 'Are you drunk? Where did you dream that one up?'

'It's true, I tell you! People round here are getting angry, they want to kill the whites! It was Shiringutira who told me a short while ago!'

Noticing how upset she was and sensing the terror in her voice and in her face, he was totally taken aback. It must be true; after all, this wasn't the first time something like this had happened. Small incidents, natural and trivial enough at the time, now seemed to be more like symptoms. There were the greedy glances in the direction of his merchandise, there were ambiguous remarks, perhaps even his own affability was a source

of trouble. He'd no idea. This was all he needed! He heaved a great sigh
of exasperation and despair.

After all that effort, after all those years of work, to be suddenly reduced
to nothing! And his poor house! Impetuously, he got up from his chair
and rushed into the bedroom to get his pistol.

'I'll kill anybody who tries to get in!' he growled.

But, as night started to fall, once the intention to attack was
confirmed, he prudently made off with his family to a safe place, just as
he had done, years before, in a similar situation. How could he confront
a horde of attackers all on his own and with scant ammunition? Honestly
and affably, his words had won for him some degree of devotion in the
hearts of the native inhabitants. But that had been in a relaxed
atmosphere of mutual confidence, in which both sides were armed only
with mutual respect. Now, however, when vengeful feelings blazed in
every heart, anything he said would be greeted with scorn. For that
reason, he preferred to take refuge some way away in the hut of a
relative of one of his servants.

In their rage, the rebels who were plotting a general uprising against
all the settlers in the region, not only plundered the house of the
wretched runaway, but they also set fire to it as an epilogue. Elsewhere,
nobody escaped death. Measured as though by the same yardstick,
concubines and servants perished with their masters. The enemy was not
just the whites, it was anybody who took up with them. So the settlers
were massacred, and their servants were massacred with them.

'Don't kill me! You can take all I possess, but please don't kill me!'
pleaded one trader, whose name was João Manuel.

His attackers, who were armed with rifles, assegais, machetes and
axes, just laughed wildly and uttered oaths accompanied by terrifying
gestures.

'I've always treated you well and been your friend! Don't kill me, look, there are my possessions, help yourselves! I'll even be your slave!' he went on, abasing himself completely.

He escaped death. But he paid dearly for his crazy desire to stay alive at all costs: painted black and always watched over, he was forced to carry out precisely those jobs that, as their master, he had ordered his servants to do.

'You, get some water!'

'Watch over the cart, I'm going to Kamutoba's house.'

Eventually, the crisis passed, and peace once more returned with the former patterns of life, just as calm periods alternate with a storm.

'Things seem to be going well now...' mused Katemo late one afternoon, sitting at his door in an easy chair.

The day was shrouding itself in dusk. The idyllic, clear-cut appearance of the woodland, the gentle shadows of which reached into his soul, melted imperceptibly away into the softness of a sigh, yet a sigh expressive of universal suffering, a foreshadowing of death. In the barnyard, goats could be heard snorting, and there rose up the single moo of an ox. The sky appeared to groan, and everything beneath it as well.

Imbued with the all-embracing melancholia, the trader drowsily reflected on his remote life out here in the bush and on all the pitfalls of the past. How grievous the voice of time was! In funereal procession, episode after episode passed before his glazed eyes, each one in its turn leaving a shrill farewell echoing down into the very depths of his soul. How much more desirable his homeland now seemed! He felt an anguished homesickness, a burning desire to see it once more! Idle dreams, alas!

Fond ambition had sent him out in hot pursuit of his fortune. But fortune had played cruel games with him, choosing to hurl him back to the point at which he had started. How many times had he had to go back and start all over again? If he'd been a villain (as so many others were), he'd have come out on top, that was for certain. But crooked dealing was something he found repugnant: he was a Christian, after all, not just because he said so but because his actions proclaimed the fact.

What an Odyssey his life had been! A life of toil and yet more toil; three times everything had been undone owing to some outbreak by the native population; that was the cross he had to bear on his progress through the bush. What of now, now that things were going well again, what new mishap would arise to cause him to fall back yet again? Alas for the place of his birth, his beloved native soil! If only there were some way to return there, to stay there for ever!

From the house there came the shrill sound of a voice. It was his woman, who was singing as she cooked. It was a plaintive, deeply mournful chant, rather than a song. Not that she was tearful about anything, her life was in no way a source of torment to her. Perhaps she was involuntarily singing a lament for her race – a race damned by the centuries, bearing the stigma of dehumanization! In consequence, this poor black woman's singing seemed less a song than a wistful lament for suffering long past.

A sudden tender sadness swept over the settler. The idea of a permanent return to Portugal evaporated: he even began to feel scorn for the idea. Though he belonged to a different people, didn't he really consider himself to be an adopted son of Africa? Didn't Africa now throb within his breast? And, as for his business, sacrosanct as it was to him after so many setbacks, didn't it represent a part of his very being? No, if he had to die, then let it be right here. Now that Africa was eating at his flesh, then it might as well eventually gnaw at his bones.

'Isn't it time for our meal, Daddy?' called one of his little children from the doorway, but in his local tongue, as was common in the bush, such being the use that the settler made of it.

By the end of the meal, who should arrive with some partridges but Valente, a trader who operated some thirty kilometres away. He was on his way home from a hunting trip. As he had already had a good bite to eat, he declined the offer of some supper. In spite of being made the guest of honour of a cask of wine, a princely privilege in that place at that time, what he really wanted at that moment, as always, was spirits.

'Damn and blast this toothache!' he complained, in mid-conversation. 'Would you mind letting me have just one more little drop of the hard stuff...'

Katemo went into the shop and came back with a glass of spirits.

'Oh hell, really! D'you think I'm some black that you have to go and bring it in a glass?' Valente complained once more.

'My dear fellow, drink as much as you like... It's just that yesterday I seemed to be constantly jumping up after drinking that stuff earlier on!'

'You'll not find me with that trouble! Stomach upsets aren't in my line. Everything else, yes, but not that!'

Fascinated by the light, a butterfly fluttered round the carbide gas-lamp that stood on the rough-hewn table. In the next room the children were already asleep.

'As for old Jacinto,' went on Katemo, 'all he needs is the smell of bad meat! He says it's with all the travelling he's done...'

Taking a long swig, Valente replied: 'He's just like the English... holding their noses while they eat partridge...'

'Hmm... Anyway, rotten meat's not for me either. Now fish... well, one's just like another. That I can tolerate. But meat that reeks like a corpse... No, thanks!'

'The worst part is starting the habit, I reckon...Still, the snag is that here we are, stuck in the back of beyond!' He took another gulp and let out a long sigh: 'Ah! I think the wretched thing's not quite so bad now, it'll pass...'

'Well, go on then, finish it off!' said his friend ironically.

'It just needs one more drop, d'you know? Yesterday it didn't bother me once.' He changed his tone: 'How about a game of cards?'

And, after his cautious sipping, the glass finally stood empty.

One night, when the children were already fast asleep, a bitter quarrel made the very rafters shake: it had started from a simple little disagreement and ended up all angry and complicated.

'Get out of here, beat it, you black she-devil!' he bellowed, in an onset of rage.

Meekly, she slunk away, servile and hurt, heading back to her native village, which was about a kilometre away. As if he understood the plight of his mistress, the cat followed her, miaowing piteously as they made their way through the hostile darkness of the forest.

Leaning out of the window, Katemo tried to calm his irritation by smoking a cigarette. Out there, on all sides, the lugubrious voices of the night sent forth their constant echo: the croaking of the frogs resembled some macabre death-rattle, the chirring of the insects was like disconsolate weeping, and the birdcalls seemed to be so many warnings. But he heard neither the frogs, nor the insects, nor the birds. In his despair, all he could hear was the storm within him.

What an appalling destiny this was, to have to put up with black women! Why had he ever set up house with a savage? Was there no woman back home capable of understanding him? What was the point of going on living in this wild spot? He suddenly felt very homesick. If only he had some white woman who could really look after him! Black women were only of any use to black men! That was it, he needed a white woman; she'd be worth more asleep than a black woman awake!

With his senses in a confused state, he mentally pictured his girlfriend going further and further away and could still hear the miaowing of the cat resounding piteously and reproachfully.

Moved by that strange farewell, he felt his rage recede, giving place to a feeling of remorse. There was no doubt, he'd behaved badly! For what reason had he driven the poor black girl out? And what a time of day to do it, dear God! After all, wasn't she the mother of his three children? And hadn't she helped him in his struggle to make a living?
Hadn't she given her all to see him through the worst periods?

His remorse drove him outdoors, to call her back.

'Kafeka! Kafeka!' he shouted, with all his might.

But she didn't answer. All that could be heard in the darkness, like souls in torment, was the long, penetrating echo of his call, borne away by the breeze. Poor woman!

'Kafeka! Kafeka!'

The same silence as before. Alone, through the vast emptiness of the night, came again the harrowing echo: 'Kafeka! Kafeka!'

In mounting and bitter anxiety, the settler ran in the direction she had taken. Why had he driven her out so brutally? His behaviour had been abominable, unforgivable.

'Kafeka! Kafeka!'

But his entreaty found no answer. The air just cast his words back again: 'Kafeka! Kafeka!'

In a torment, he wracked his brains to think where she could be. The tears that she had shed when she left now seemed to burn within him, seemed to relegate him to a position lower than that of savages. For all his brutishness, the savage would have been more humane, would have resolved things more calmly.

In his confused mind, he saw no longer her but the blacks in general, sold like cattle, exported like cargo. It was because of their very backwardness, he thought, that the civilized man committed such excesses. They were a hapless race! Why did the Almighty cause such inequality between men?

'Kafeka! Kafeka!'

But Kafeka gave no answer, only the night once more repeated: 'Kafeka! Kafeka!'

He was a monster! To think that he'd driven her out like that, just because she was black! When she was the mother of his children! Her tears were now flowing deep within him!

'Kafeka! Kafeka!'

'Kafeka! Kafeka!' he shouted, redoubling his efforts, beside himself with anguish.

The wind continued its funeral march. Its sombre rhythm chilled the settler, as though one of her laments had pierced his heart. All around him, everything seemed to be weeping: the trees, the grass, the insects. Everything was weeping, every single thing, because remorse itself was crying out in his very soul. He must find her, must take her back home. She was a very humble person, she didn't deserve such harsh treatment. His helpmate, the mother of his children, she had to come back to him that very night. It was that miaow, a miaow that wasn't a miaow but a heart-rending farewell. He called a greeting at the entrance to a conical hut.

A log fire was giving out sorry comfort to a huddled group of men and women.

'Is that you, Katemo? How are you?' several voices asked, in a familiar tone.

'Yes, it's me. I've come to take your daughter back.'

'Ha!' broke in her mother, scornfully, 'but didn't you drive her out?'

'Yes, I did, but that nonsense is all over. Now I've come to take her home. Come on, Kafeka, let's be off home, all right?'

Crackling feebly, the wood of the fire filled the hut with smoke. But nobody paid any heed, smoke had already penetrated deep down into their being.

'Oh, come on, now! Why won't you get up? Look, it's time we left! I'm not angry with you any more! Don't you want to live with me any longer?' he went on, in answer to her indifference.

'Katemo, what you did, well, it wasn't right! If you wanted to send your girl away, then at least you should have waited till morning. But, at this time, when it's dark, to send her out alone, that's not right, Katemo! A man is a man, and a woman is a woman! Don't you realize there are wild animals our there among the trees? Really, Katemo! What you did wasn't right!'

Though these words came from the mouth of a man without any education, the settler made no attempt to argue against the rebuke. He had behaved really badly, yes, he had. And when reproached for it, what good was it to answer back? Anybody with a regard for justice should be prepared to apply it to himself, as well as to other people.

'You're quite right, Kambundo. The trouble is, when people get angry, they often do crazy things, don't you think so?'

Close to the hut, a hen that was nestling with its brood, let out a hollow cackle. The other hens slept elsewhere, in a conical hut of their own, which, because of wild animals, stood on stilts.

But the man didn't reply, plunging back once more into fervent puffing of his pipe. What the white man said was true. When people got angry, they did crazy things.

'Come along, Kafeka, your children are waiting for you at home. Let's be off, don't be angry any more!' he insisted.

His voice was gentle and reached her heart. It was his usual voice, not the angry voice of a short while ago. She still felt resentful but was sorry for her white man. He was a good white man, really, poor fellow! But she still didn't get up.

'Up you get, Kafeka,' urged her mother, 'your man isn't angry any more. Off you go! Go back home, back to your children.'

The fire was now smiling, nervously. The smoke didn't stop, though, and went on adding to the soot that covered the inside of the wretched hut. The crickets, cri... cri... cri... went on filling the night air with their mournful noise, in a cadence that rose and fell.

The settler advanced gently towards his loved one and equally gently pulled at her arm: 'Come on, let's go home, now, our children can't be left on their own. All right?'

With the sudden movement, the cat, which was curled up in her lap, jumped up and started purring. Half sadly, half smiling, Kafeka simply murmured: 'Hello, white man!...' and she followed him home, followed in turn by... the tender miaow.

WHICH HURTS MORE?

From a circle of skipping children, in the midst of which another waddled about in a squatting position, there arose a lively chorus:

Watch out for the bird, watch out for the bird!
Oooh!
Watch out for the bird!

'Ouch, I've been caught!' squealed one of the links in the chain, trying to work free from the make-believe bird of prey in the middle.

The rhythm of the chanting became slower, as the circle inquired: 'By what animal?'

'By the bird.'

'Break free...'

'I can't, it's holding me tight.'

Still circling round with the same urgency, his playmates advised: 'Tell your relatives, then.'

As though to exorcise his attacker, and egged on by the others, the poor victim began to chant the following words:

My father's away,
oooh!
He doesn't know about the bird!

My mother's away,
oooh!
She doesn't know about the bird!

... ...

Because of a childish prank,
oooh!
I've been caught by the bird!

Fate marked me out,
oooh!
to get caught by the bird!

Spare me from the evil omen,
oooh!
I want to get free of the bird!

The accursed bird let go of its prey, and the song began again as the children went on skipping in a circle. Sitting on the ground, an older group of children were amusing one another with stories and guessing games.

'Guess this one!' called out one boy.

'Guess what?' they all chorused, in the traditional reply.

'A sparrow hiding behind a dunghill...'

'That's your nail behind your finger.'

Then a girl tried out her knowledge: 'Guess this one!'

'Guess what?' called out the others.

'It's a red basket with an *andua*'s feather...'

'That's to show love in one's face, as well as feeling it in one's heart.'

'Guess this one!' broke in another participant, in an impish tone of voice.

'Guess what?'

'What are my mother-in-law's breasts?'

Hoots and guffaws accompanied the answer: 'Two pieces of rope.'

'Somebody tell a story,' suggested Muongo, who was the most appealing of the girls, but also the most aloof.

This was immediately taken up by Mukilango, one of her would-be boyfriends: 'Which story do you want?'

'Any story! Any story!' chorused the group.

They all sat attentively as the fable began:

Once upon a time, Mr Elephant, Mr Lion, Mrs Panther, Mrs Buffalo and several other animals all had their own fields, where they grew maize and sweet potato. But they couldn't eat anything, because they had no fire to cook by. So they just drank.

Nearby, in a vast tree that was full of fruit, lived Mr Lizard. From time to time, he would climb down from his tree and go and chat to the others. One day, Mr Elephant spoke to his companions about him: 'Our friend Lizard is always very contented with his lot, he never complains of being hungry, and he doesn't go about looking for fire like we do. I'm sure he must get plenty to eat. As for his food, well, I'm looking straight at it, it's that stuff up in the tree, not to mention what's fallen to the ground. Why don't we go and ask the Creator the truth of the situation, then we can put an end to our suffering.'

They all thought it was a good plan, and Mr Elephant was the first to set off. In the Beyond, he told the Creator about their wretched hunger and their misgivings about what Mr Lizard ate. The Creator answered him as follows: 'Yes, it can be eaten, and the tree is called Tree-Tree, Sorcerer-Zelembwa, Muzelembwa, Sorcerer-Tree. Sing its name to yourself on your way home, because it's so long that you might otherwise forget it. And when you get there, the tree will come crashing down, in answer to your singing. And then you can eat.'

Busily concentrating on this advice – Tree-Tree, Sorcerer-Zelembwa, Muzelembwa, Sorcerer-Tree – , Mr Elephant set off on his way home. But Mr Lizard, who knew about what was going on, no sooner caught sight of him in the distance than he went to meet him and invited him to dance. Poor Mr Elephant did so, and thereby forgot the magic words.

The next to go was Mr Lion. The Creator gave him a warm welcome and gave him the same advice. Feeling pleased with himself, Mr Lion made his way home, repeating the magic words: Tree-Tree, Sorcerer-Zelembwa, Muzelembwa, Sorcerer-Tree. But, lo and behold, rascally Mr Lizard was there to invite him to dance and thus get him all muddled.

Animal after animal, they all fell into the same trap, until, finally, Mr Tortoise undertook to make the journey to the Beyond. But his companions were outraged at the very idea and gave him a thorough thrashing.

'Really, have you no respect for your betters? *We* didn't have any success, and now you, who can hardly walk, how d'you think you can do any better?'

Nevertheless, Mr Monkey protested indignantly at this: 'Let him go! What harm can there be in that? Is it his fault we were all so forgetful?'

So Mr Tortoise set off in his customary dead-slow fashion. The Creator gave him a good hearing and even granted him the grace to be able to resist everything.

On the way home, he made light of the possible temptations. Ah yes, Mr Lizard could kill him, if he felt like it, but he'd recover and go on chanting the magic words. Mr Lizard could hack him to pieces and bury him, but he'd recover and go on chanting the magic words. Mr Lizard could eat him and then turn him into excrement. But he'd recover and go on chanting the magic words. And that's just what happened. He emerged victorious, and the tree came crashing down.

Out of envy, his fellow-animals ate up all the fruit and gave him nothing but insults and another beating. But Mr Monkey, who felt sorry for him, saved him a morsel or two.

Days passed, and then hunger returned. Deep within them, the dire need to find fire had returned. Where were they to get it from? Where?

One morning, Mr Elephant noticed a wisp of smoke curling upwards from the other side of a mountain. He pointed it out to his companions.

'Just look at that! Where there's smoke, there's fire!'

The others took a long look and agreed with him. It was smoke, there was no doubt about it. So Mr Elephant decided to set off and ask the fortunate person, whoever it was, to let him have a live ember for his fire. He was making his way down the far side of the mountain when he heard someone call out.

'Who's that who dares to climb the Cricket's mountain? Look, I ate the buffalo all at one go, and two mouthfuls are enough to eat up the elephant! Come on, then – I'll fix *you*!'

Mr Elephant was terrified, he didn't know that voice. He beat a hasty retreat and told the others what had happened.

Mr Lion was most surprised: he'd go and see who this bogey was. But, on the other side of the mountain, the same threat was repeated: 'Who's that who dares to climb the Cricket's mountain? Look, I ate the buffalo all at one go, and two mouthfuls are enough to eat up the elephant! Come on, then – I'll fix *you*!'

Scared stiff, he turned tail. And, just as before, everybody had a try at it. And, just as before, Mr Tortoise was once more given a thrashing. But off he went, thanks to the intervention of Mr Monkey.

'Who's that who dares to climb the Cricket's mountain? Look, I ate the buffalo all at one go, and two mouthfuls are enough to eat up the elephant! Come on, then – I'll fix *you*!'

Mr Tortoise refused to be intimidated by such bravado and just kept plodding on. On and on he went, while Mr Cricket, in his turn, went on snarling.

'Who're you, then?' asked Mr Tortoise, once he got close to his lair.

Mr Cricket was somewhat taken aback.

'Ah! It's Uncle Tortoise! Come on in, I didn't realize it was you,' he said, offering him a seat.

'Of course it's me!'

'What brings you here?'

'I've come in search of a live ember; back there we've nothing to cook by and we're all terribly famished!'

'Oh, so that's all! D'you know what, whenever I heard all those footsteps approaching, I was frightened out of my mind. What'd become of me, if friend Elephant went and put his great foot on top of my den? So you see, uncle, I had to bluster away, and that was the great hullabaloo that you heard...'

They both had a good laugh. While they waited for some sweet potatoes to get nicely roasted, they chatted on in the most friendly fashion.

'Very well, then, but don't go and say I was the one who gave it to you, or they'll get their revenge by killing me. I know: say you didn't see anybody, so you just came in and helped yourself to the fire, how about that?'

Such was Mr Cricket's scheme, as he busied himself getting some live embers ready. But Mr Tortoise hid the truth when he got back, for fear of another scolding.

'There we are, didn't we say so? The very idea that, if *we* couldn't get an ember, *you* would!' guffawed Mr Elephant.

But, on the quiet, Mr Tortoise called over his friend, Mr Monkey: 'D'you want to know something? I've brought some fire. But keep it a secret. Come on, let's go to your field and do some cooking.'

Their companions soon noticed the smoke and were furious; they came rushing up and gave poor Mr Tortoise another tremendous thrashing.

'They'll pay for what they've done to me!' he said to his friend, confidentially. 'In a short while, I'm off to my pond. There'll be some accounts to settle there, you'll see. But be careful when you go for a drink! Don't do it in their company but clamber up a baobab tree and wait for me to call you.'

At dusk, as usual, all the animals went along to slake their thirst. Mr Elephant was the first to approach. But there was nothing there! Instead of water he encountered something hard. He prodded it with his foot. Still nothing! So he trumpeted an entreaty:

> *Water, oh water, I'm going to plunge in my trunk,*
> *with tremendous force, with tremendous force!*
> *Aah, mother of mine,*
> *I'm dying of thirst!*

> *Water, oh water, I'm going to plunge in my trunk,*
> *with tremendous force, with tremendous force!*
> *Aah, father of mine,*
> *I'm dying of thirst!*

With that, he plunged in his trunk and crunch! his great snout got stuck: it was a great sheet of marble and it not only covered the whole pool but it was also the same colour as water.

Next, Mr Lion arrived. He also came upon the great stone and, in turn, invoked the names of his parents. The same fate befell him and then all the others, right down to the last one. Then, suddenly, craack! the great stone shattered, and they were all smashed to pieces. Only Mr Monkey, because he'd been fair, escaped the punishment and became a firm friend of Mr Tortoise.

'That's the end of the story,' concluded Mukilango. 'It's up to you to say whether it was good or bad.'

'It was a good one,' everybody shouted.

Then the children formed up in single file and trotted off in an orderly fashion, each one touching the one in front; anybody knocking into or colliding with anybody else was eliminated from the game. As they made their way along, they chanted the following words in rhythmic accompaniment:

I went, I went, I went,
I went to my mother-in-law's,
and there I found a buffalo,
who was busy having a shave!

Why shouldn't I? said the buffalo,
why shouldn't I have a shave?
Am I supposed to be like the sparrow,
that nestles up in the palm tree?
Am I supposed to be like the hen,
that scratches about in her coop?

Why shouldn't I? said the hen,
why shouldn't I scratch about in my coop?
D'you expect me to go outside,
so that the wild cat can catch me?

Why shouldn't I? said the wildcat,
why shouldn't I catch hens?
D'you think I do it for fun?
It's because I'm hungry, hungry, hungry!

Among the grown-ups, someone was accompanying a group of dancers on a string instrument, the *bwetete*. He sang as he plucked away, and the dancers all joined in. Their singing had a tragic theme, which reflected itself in the tender melancholy of their voices.

It was the story of a drowning. Overcome by the sad news, a poor mother laments the death of her two daughters, who had gone sailing in a canoe, along with some other girls. On the occasion of the disaster, they had all been thrown into the river, but her two daughters were the only ones to lose their lives. And it was all their own fault. Without their realizing it, they were both chasing the same man, despite their mother's warnings about his rascally nature, which they didn't heed. Alas, she even felt a shudder of shame! If only they'd listened to her advice, none of this would have happened. And so, Kashindanda, you died within sight of your younger sister, and she died in sight of you!

Oh Kashindanda, I did warn you!
Now imagine my sense of shame!
Oh Kashindanda!

So sang the dancers, as they jerked their hips in time with the seductive rhythm.

'That bottom of yours will start a knife-fight one day,' said Mukilango, trying to flirt with Muongo.

Putting on a sulky look, she retorted: 'Huh, who wants you, with your hyena face?'

'Who d'you think? Why, you, of course! I've already noticed that you fancy me.'

'Spare me that evil omen!'

'Don't be like that to me, you'll cry for me yet!'

In the end, pretending to be disconsolate, Mukilango drew public attention to his feigned plight: 'I say, listen, everybody. From now on, my name is to be "The pain of sorrow is greater than that of a knife wound".'

'All right, then, and I'll be "The pain of a knife wound is greater than that of sorrow",' reacted Kimavo.

'What? The pain of a knife wound is greater than that of sorrow? Are you sure you're feeling all right?'

'Why not? If somebody knifes you, don't you shout and scream?'

'Oh, the knife wound hurts, of course, but that's only the flesh; on the other hand, sorrow hurts all the way down to the heart itself.'

With the clash of the two ideas, each boy argued all the harder in favour of his saying. The dispute electrified the listeners, as if forming two currents. Examples were put forward, and incidents were recounted in support of their arguments. But there was no shifting of individual opinion, as their fervour drew snorts of derision from either side.

All this took place in the young people's play area, by the light of grass bonfires, while the older people, paying due court to their chief, chatted away under the shade of the tree by his royal hut, lit by the more effective glow of blazing wooden torches. It was in the time of Chief Kimone Kya Songa., in the lands of Kissama, many, many years ago.

The following day, chatting to Kimone Kya Songa, one of the elders reported on the argument. He had heard it by accident, as he made his way through the youngsters' play area.

As an idea took shape in his mind, the chief chuckled: 'I'll show young Mukilango that the pain of a knife wound is greater than that of sorrow!'

'Quite so, the lad is cunning, though, and we'll have to show him where he's wrong.'

The chief was as good as his word and persuaded two other chiefs from nearby territories (Kikulimone and Bombe were their names) to come and see him.

Taking counsel with them on this unusual topic, he asked them: 'Don't you think this youngster has a heart full of cunning?'

His colleagues agreed; indeed, the boy was entertaining rather dangerous ideas.

A court usher was dispatched, bearing the sceptre, to summon Mukilango.

'Our noble chief has sent for you,' he announced.

Mukilango, who was working on his patch of land, stopped what he was doing and, somewhat apprehensively, went along with the usher. The staff of office, which was only used for official matters, was ample confirmation of the summons. But what could it be about? Not even the court bailiff knew.

Beneath the shade of the tree that stands by the chieftain's residence, preparations were being made to proceed to a verdict. Seated on thrones, with crowns on their heads, were the three chiefs, while their ministers had taken up their places on benches, holding their staffs of office.

'So the pain of sorrow is greater than that of a knife wound?' said Kimone Kya Songa, beginning the questioning.

Mukilango, who was squatting down in front of them with his hands at his sides, was most ill at ease and too overcome with fright to answer. The people, who had all assembled at the blasts blown on the ceremonial buffalo horn, were likewise squatting in a great semicircle and in low whispers commented on the curious nature of the question. Meanwhile, one of the elders, coming to the rescue, repeated the inquiry: 'Our noble chief is asking if the pain of sorrow is greater than that of a knife wound...'

Like a flash of lightning, comprehension broke through into Mukilango's mind. Ah yes! Now he remembered yesterday's argument: 'Yes, great lord, the pain of sorrow is greater than that of a knife wound,' he confirmed, still partly stunned.

After turning to smile knowingly at his companions, Kimone Kya Songa addressed Mukilango in a somewhat mocking tone: 'Very well, then. Now I'm going to prove to you that the pain of sorrow *isn't* greater than that of a knife wound.'

Terrified at this, Mukilango humbly replied: 'Noble lord, it's just a saying, as you know...'

'Yes, indeed, but not for one of your age, you rascal! If you have thoughts like that now, when you're nothing but a worthless boy, what are you going to think of later on? You're not only a good-for-nothing but you also show signs of becoming positively dangerous; and so, as an example to others like you, so that they shall all come to treat me with due respect, you are about to learn the saying that the pain of a knife wound is greater than that of sorrow.' With that, he gave the order to several guards to tie up Mukilango there and then and to subject him to a series of knife wounds.

The assembled crowd had little option but to support this and clapped in reverent approval. 'Quite right, noble lord, quite right!'

Night was furtively approaching. In the gloom of dusk, the great tree by the royal residence loomed over the groans of pain that arose from below. The smoke from the fires soared beyond, bearing with it a vast anguish, which was borne far away on the wings of the west wind.

In the immense peace of a night of stars, Mukilango, scarred by many knife wounds, let out moan after moan, as evidence in favour of the saying which ran contrary to his own.

'Poor, poor boy!' thought Muongo sadly. 'And it's all because of me...!' She felt deeply sorry for him in his plight.

Months passed away. One day, there was consternation in the chief's residence: Kandalo, the princess, was pregnant.

'But how did you get a great belly like that?' asked her mother.

'What d'you mean, great belly? How could I possibly, if I haven't got a man?'

But the cruel obviousness of her pregnancy contradicted the vehemence of her denials. How had it come about? After all the trouble and care taken, she'd turned out like that! If the old customs hadn't been observed, then it would have been hardly surprising if Kandalo had got into that condition. But, on the contrary, the princess was always chaperoned. Wherever she went, her mother, one of her stepmothers or some other woman whom the family trusted, would constantly shadow her, even when she simply went out to answer the demands of nature.

'But I've never been alone with a man, you all know that perfectly well!' swore Kandalo.

Yet, with monotonous, hammer-like insistence, the accusation came back in constant rejoinder: 'How d'you explain your great belly, then?'

The chief, once informed of the surprising news by his principal wife, was enraged at this affront to his honour. If Kandalo was never left alone, how could she have become pregnant?

'You haven't looked after her properly, any of you! What a scandal! A princess of my house, pregnant! The wretch who did this will pay dearly for it!'

He harried his daughter with his questions. But she stood her ground and stuck firmly to her denials. With her constant chaperones, how could she get with child?

Kimone Kya Songa summoned a meeting of fellow chiefs and of his ministers, to hear their views. But the burden of the charges fell on him. If Kandalo was always so carefully chaperoned, if Kandalo always slept in her father's room, if Kandalo swore she didn't have a man, then who could have done it? He and he alone.

At this suggestion of an incestuous relationship, Kimone Kya Songa was overcome by a great sadness and fell severely ill as a result.

'Sorcerer!' people muttered to one another. 'Why on earth did you sink to such depths?'

Kimone Kya Songa was soon within sight of death. When he heard what happened, Mukilango went along to the royal residence and asked to be allowed to speak to an assembly of the elders, as he had something important to tell them.

On the appointed day, in front of an assembly that included the two neighbouring chiefs, all the ministers and a great crowd of other people, Mukilango asked the following question: 'Do you all remember, gentlemen, when I was given a series of knife wounds for saying that the pain of sorrow is greater than that of a knife wound?'

A great murmur of voices went up in reply. 'Yes, indeed, we remember it very well,' answered Kikulimone.

Greatly intrigued, Bombe pressed further: 'Why do you mention that now?'

'Because now the opposite is happening: on account of his daughter, the noble and respected Kimone Kya Songa, who had me punished for using that saying as a nickname, is now dying of sorrow. Don't you all agree that this is the case?'

Another murmur arose from the crowd, though it was one of approval. The chiefs and the elders exchanged puzzled glances.

'In fact, I was the one who made his daughter pregnant!' added Mukilango, pausing to beat his chest with his fist.

'You! It was you, young man?!'

'Yes, gentlemen, I'm the one who did it. I did it to prove to the noble Kimone Kya Songa that the pain of sorrow is greater than that of a knife wound.'

'But, if Kandalo was always chaperoned, how did you manage that?' inquired Kikulimone.

'I did it with *banze*...[1] even with her father and mother in the room, I was able to enter with ease. All I had to do was puff, and the door would open. With the *banze* always in my mouth, I did what I wanted, and Kandalo didn't even notice. Now I want the noble Kimone Kya Songa to know all about this. As you can see, gentlemen, I've recovered from my knife wounds, but my chief has not recovered, because his wounds are in his very heart.'

Muongo, who had begun to be fond of Mukilango from the time he had been tortured, now felt herself to be very inferior. Mukilango had been right in saying that one day she'd be sorry and weep for him...

---

[1] *Banze* is a magical compound of certain powdered leaves, which, if placed in a wad between cheek and gum, allegedly confers mysterious properties upon the power of thought: doors open at a mere puff, women can be taken without their even noticing... and so forth (TN).

The elders deliberated and then sent for their ailing chief, who was brought to them, supported on the arms of two guards. When the revelation was made known to him, he let out a whimper of joy and, in a faint voice, asked for time to get better, so that then he could decide on the matter once and for all.

He recovered quickly, now that his moral burden had been lifted from him, and summoned another assembly. Having repeated the story of what Mukilango had done, he turned to him and said: 'Young man, you have taught me a lesson that I deserved. Now you shall marry Kandalo and reign in my stead.'

THE CURSE

That morning, on returning home, Mussoko called out in glee: 'Aunt, just see how lucky I've been! I've found a package, with quite a bit of money in it!'

'Don't shout, they'll be able to hear you outside! Bring it into the bedroom,' urged her aunt. She was sitting on a bench, steadily cleaning her teeth with an impregnated stick.

Mussoko's great-aunt, who was sweeping the yard and had a similar stick in her mouth, heard the intriguing exchange and came hurrying in. 'What's all this, then?' she chimed in.

'*Kia ngi kola... a ngi kuata... bu dibebe... dia nguari!...*' (I'm unlucky... they caught me... in a trap... set for a partridge!...), trilled a dove from its nest nearby.

Once behind closed doors, hearts pumping, the three of them sat together on the iron bedstead, nervously counting and checking what Mussoko had found. Two hundred and ten escudos! My! God is great, he doesn't forget sinners!

Her great-aunt was the first to offer advice: 'Not a word about this to anybody! You've seen nothing, d'you hear? With this tidy sum, Mussoko, you'll be able to buy your own little place to live in.'

'No, great-aunt! What do I want a house for? Let's buy some nice clothes... some jewellery... and, then, if there's enough money left, I could buy a sewing machine...'

'Yes, you can buy a few little things for yourself... But to have one's own home is far better than renting one... Don't be silly!' her aunt objected.

'But what I want is to be well dressed, not own a house! Am I not supposed to enjoy my money?' She jumped up, a bit giddy, and lurched a few steps from the *massemba* dance, feeling some of her enthusiasm beginning to ebb away.

Her great-aunt grinned, clapped her hands together and clicked her fingers. 'There you are, you see! Money just drives people crazy!'

'Go on, dance around, then. Your guardian spirits have obviously been looking after you...', joked her aunt in turn.

A little while later, one of the neighbours alarmed the whole area with her clamour. 'Has anybody found two hundred and ten escudos? If anyone has, please let me have them back, because I'm the one who's lost them! Hello! Has anybody found my money? You who work, you know how the poor have to make sacrifices, don't hide my money away when I'm looking for it! I've lost two hundred and ten escudos! Who's found them? If only I could see where they've got to! The hard of heart always get a hard grave! Listen, will you! I'm calling to everybody!'

In an excitement born of fear and better instincts, Mussoko thought of handing the money back to its owner. If she'd been unaware of who it was, as she had been till then, then it would have been different. But now... knowing who it was, how could she fail to give it back to her? Especially seeing she was a friend.

'Aunt, listen, I'm going to give Donana her money back. Can't you hear what she's saying? The hard of heart will always get a hard grave, she says!' said Mussoko in an excited whisper.

But, like an impregnable redoubt, her aunt perfidiously raised objections: 'What d'you mean, give it back? You didn't steal the money, you found it in the street, didn't you? So it's yours, then! What's there to be afraid of?'

'Don't throw good luck away!' added her great-aunt, in support. 'Finding isn't stealing. Finders, keepers, I say. No harm can come to you, so don't be so stupid!'

The men and women of the area greatly commiserated with poor distraught Donana as she trudged through the streets, crying out piteously. All that money! Poor woman! But who could have found it? Not them, they'd found nothing at all. But could anybody really be so heartless as to profit from somebody else's suffering? No, no, on once hearing her cries, nobody would keep such a thing quiet. It would be inhuman to hold on to as much money as that when its owner was begging out loud for it to be given back! No, no, nobody could commit such a sin, every one of them knew just how hard life was.

'Listen, Donana, where did you actually lose the money?' asked groups of passers-by, as they swarmed round her in the street.

Repeating the same sad rigmarole over and over again, she explained: 'I've no idea where! Early this morning I was on my usual way down to the Kwanza to pay some money I owed for some cigarettes and to look for some more business. When I got to Alta Station, God help me! I noticed I'd no longer got the money. I scurried back home, searching on the ground the whole way. Once home, I ransacked everything, bags, drawers, clothes. No sign! There wasn't a nook or a cranny I didn't rummage through. I even tried the mattresses. Nothing!' With a deep sigh, she went on: 'Just think, all those hardships, all that hunger and danger I went through out in the bush, and then all those days on end I've spent selling in the street, putting up with grumpy customers, and where has it got me? To this sorry pass where I suddenly have nothing to show for all those years of sweat! Ooh!' She wrung her hands in despair. 'I've been calling out everywhere. I've tried Ingombota till I was exhausted. And then in Bungo. And the same in Maianga. I'm worn out! I've tried the fish market and the meat market and I'm worn out, worn out, worn out! I've called out everywhere! Not a soul has come forward with the money!'

The women who gathered round all joined in the chorus of lamentation. Whoever had taken the money, why, why wouldn't they hand it back? How could anybody listen to somebody else sob like that, pouring out her heart, and not hand the money over? Just how heartless could people be? The only excuse could ever be if nobody claimed it!

'*Kie, kie, kie, kiu ki tukila!*' (It's yours, it's yours, it's yours, but they still turn against you!), shrilled a little grey bird with a white breast, as it waddled along the branch of a mulemba tree.

Days of anguish went by. Luanda itself seemed to be overcome by the calamity and by the sorrowing woman's cries. They were all children of the same wretchedness. How could any one of them carry in his breast the burning guilt of such a despicable act? Anybody who knew how hard money was to come by, who earned his daily bread by the sweat of his brow, who slept the uneasy sleep of those who suffer all the perils of life could never turn so flint-like at the sound of such desperate appeals. No, no, they'd never do such a thing, one poor man understands another! Whether they spent their lives washing or cooking in the houses of the wealthy, hawking in the streets or just working in their own homes, life never ceased to torment them. If they worked for others, they were forever humiliated by their masters, they had to listen to their complaints, put up with their demands and go without normal comforts, all for *their* benefit. If they worked independently, there was no shortage of hardships and troubles, it meant so often an empty belly and God knows what difficulties, just to earn a crust.

The news had spread all over the city and was circulating again in the original quarters, not this time with a note of grief and complaint, but with a harsher, more threatening tone.

'I've called out for the money I lost, and nobody has opened his heart. Now listen and listen well. Don't say tomorrow I'm some sort of witch, but I'm going to call down a curse! D'you all hear? A curse! Pay attention now, don't complain later. The one who shall bear the curse is as good as dead! Anyone who washes him dies as well! Anyone who cuts his hair dies as well! Anyone who cuts his nails dies as well! Anyone who dresses him dies as well! Anyone who goes to be present at his death dies as well! Anyone who bewails his passing dies as well!'

'Be off with you with your evil intentions,' muttered several women, though recognizing her deeply felt reasons for saying what she did.

Just as superstitiously, others added, with a bitter smile: 'Let the curse fall on the one who made off with someone else's money!'

Mothers, some of whom carried their younger children on their backs in a cloth, made up their minds to check carefully through everything to do with their offspring. Sometimes, who knows, they could find money and be secretly spending it on sweets and other fripperies.

'The child is brother to the fool,' intoned an old woman, reinforcing the mothers' intentions.

Jangling amid the heat of the afternoon, the bells of the church dedicated to Our Lady of Mount Carmel proclaimed the entry of another infant into the bosom of the Faith. Outside, an urchin, indifferent to the growing seedbed of horror, was fancifully singing in time with the chimes.

The portent of death, however, was spreading everywhere, thrusting a terrible sense of fatality into people's souls. Who on earth could have found the money? Away with this curse, away with it! Oh heart of stone, why don't you reveal yourself?

Mussoko was more terrified than anybody else and was filled with the growing sense of alarm. In spite of the objections of her two relatives, her neighbour's laments, repeated over and over again in her house nearby, echoed tenaciously in her ears: 'You who work, you who know how the poor have to make sacrifices, don't hide my money away when I'm looking for it!' After her early exaltation, she was now beginning to feel the effects of a spiritual collapse. Fine clothes, captivating jewellery, heady pleasures, everything came crashing down in a great cataclysm. She had spoken to her aunts once more about handing over the money. But they'd retorted that she shouldn't be so foolish as to even think of it and dissuaded her just as before. But now, under the threat of the curse, she reasoned that she would really have to give up her find, whether they wanted her to or not.

'Aunt,' she urged, 'aunt, have you heard what Donana is saying now?'

'Of course I have. She can call down curses as much as she likes. Let her get on with it!'

'But all that business of curses is no mere joke,' replied Mussoko, now in a great panic.

At this point, her great-aunt, who was equally in no mood to abandon the unexpected gains, grew irritated at this obstinate outbreak of scruple of the sort she had already so much heard on all sides.

'Really! You as well! Is the money starting to burn your hands, then? Just let her chatter on, it's all just to frighten people! I wasn't born yesterday!'

'But, great-aunt...'

'Oh, get on with you! All that panic for what? If you'd stolen the money, very well, then you'd suffer as a result. But you didn't, you picked it up in the street...'

Her aunt joined in again, vehemently: 'There's only one word for it! She's just telling *lies*, she's not going to do anything! Going to call down a curse, is she? Where is she going to do it, eh? Don't you go and hand that money over, you've had a spot of good luck!' she snorted. 'Really! The very idea! Just suppose *she*'d found the money, d'you reckon she'd hand it back? Well, *do* you?' By way of an answer to her own question, she pressed down her lower left eyelid with her index finger.

Morally beaten once again, Mussoko weakly accepted the arguments as before. But, poor soul! Within her breast she couldn't help feeling it was a crime, a crime that was consuming her in great tongues of fire. Surely it was a wretched moment when she'd found the money. What good was it to her, if she found it so mortifying? Her great-aunt might well ask if it was burning her hands! Of course it was burning her, but not her hands, rather her heart, her very life! 'I'm going to call down a curse! D'you all hear? A curse!' That voice, how it frightened her! And yet it was their own neighbour, one of their friends, who was crying out like that! What evil relatives she had, and what evil friends they were! There was a lot of truth in the old saying: 'I may look like bread on the outside, but inside me all I've got is cotton.'

'I've called out for the money I lost, and nobody has opened his heart. Now listen and listen well. Don't say tomorrow I'm some sort of witch, but I'm going to call down a curse! D'you all hear? A curse! Pay attention now, don't complain later. The one who shall bear the curse is as good as dead! Anyone who washes him dies as well! Anyone who cuts his hair dies as well! Anyone who cuts his nails dies as well! Anyone who dresses him dies as well! Anyone who goes to be present at his death dies as well! Anyone who bewails his passing dies as well!' For Donana still went round and round, constantly repeating her threat.

That night, Mussoko, perhaps because of the reactions she had provoked during the day, had a redoubled and courageous impulse: she would go and give the money back to its owner. Feverishly she left the house. What point was there in informing her aunt and great-aunt? They'd only break her resolve yet again.

With the sum of money secured inside her clothing, she blundered through the darkness. It was broken only by the sounds of fleeting voices and the incessant chirring of night insects. Donana's house was right next to hers, but her feet, in secret obedience to her subconscious, kept dragging her off in the opposite direction. Half relieved, half fearful, she kept up a steady conversation with herself. Now what was she to say to her? How could she begin? By asking her whether the money had turned up? How then would she contrive to give her the money? Yes, how would she explain herself? After several days had passed, wouldn't it seem disgraceful not to be doing it till then?

Amid all these reflections, she suddenly found herself at Donana's door. Should she go in or not? And what pretext did she have? What, indeed! Had she the nerve to go through with it? Alas, no, she hadn't, she hadn't!

This time, not because of her two relatives, but because of her own timidity, she was once again beaten. It was shameful, a disgrace! The wretched, miserable money had robbed her of all peace of mind!

Appeals had been made, and then threats. But without result. Despite all the publicity, the money was lost in anonymity. There was nothing for it but the revenge of death! There was no way that Donana was going to resign herself to suffering such an appalling loss, while someone else, brutally indifferent, got the benefit of all those years of work and vexation, no way at all! Whoever it was, that person must have heard her, her laments had been heard everywhere. There wasn't a soul who could have failed to hear her. For a whole week now, through every quarter of the city, her voice had been heard, first with a beggar's wail and then in a tone of wild menace. She had promised to call down a curse and call down a curse she would. Pity? Not a bit of it! Why should she feel any pity? The person who'd kept her money presumably hadn't felt any sympathy for her in her plight. The hard of heart always get a hard grave!

In quest of an unbreakable curse, Donana went off to the Ambriz area. There, according to repute, lived witchdoctors versed in the art of calling down curses. By using spells, known as *jimbambi*, which involved states of the weather, they would cause the downfall of the accursed scoundrel at the very height of the bad weather to come. And that would be that.

'I come to seek contact with our forefathers and ancestors. Please cause the *jimbambi* to take vengeance on the one who found the money that I have lost. With your powers, please get our forefathers and ancestors to act as soon as possible,' she begged, directing her words at a witchdoctor who could rouse such avenging spirits.

She went into the room of the holy *dilombe* or spirits, whose images and emblems were kept in special baskets; falling to her knees, she angrily pounded the earth floor with her hands and, amid sobs, unleashed her vengeful curses. 'Oh gods of justice, Honji, Vunji and Mwene-Kongo, oh great gods of the World Beyond, I come to beseech your help. Because of a sum of money that I lost, I cried out in many places for a full week. But nobody, nobody at all, answered my pleas. Those with eyes merely saw me. Those with ears merely heard me. Oh forefathers and ancestors, if the one who found the money is from some distant place and did not hear my call, then let nothing befall him. But if he heard and has kept quiet, then I urge you to cut him down as though you were carving him in the market. Let the one who found the money die, and also whoever feeds him! Let all those die who wash his corpse, or cut his nails, or cut his hair or dress him, or who bewail his passing! Let them all die, all of them, each and every one, because they all heard me, but not one of them opened his heart!'

The sorcerer took a deer's horn full of powders and blew a blast on it towards the east and then another towards the west. Out into space he intoned the words of her petition, first in one direction, then in the other.

'Remember, take care whenever there is a death! Don't blunder in, don't utter any laments! Always recall the words you have chosen, the *jimbambi* are not to be trifled with,' was his solemn warning.

She was greatly encouraged. Soon, borne by the rains, the spell would come to fruition. The evildoer would never laugh at her now: into a hard grave he would fall, in the hardness of his heart. Was she a witch? No. How could anyone call her that? Hadn't she given warning of her intent? Yet who had come forward? Nobody. No, she hadn't behaved like a witch: sorcerers don't give advance warning, they deal out death out of envy. But there was no envy in her case, not one bit. To tell the truth, death wasn't about to be dealt out, it had been sought. Sought after by the guilty party who had scorned her cries. Now let him suffer the consequences.

Mussoko had felt ill for days. In spite of the careful treatment received at home, there was no let-up in her illness: high temperature, constant shooting pains, even spitting blood.

'Shouldn't we take advice from a medicine man?' suggested the great-aunt, as they watched over her, already apprehensive about Donana's spells. The aunt agreed, yawning with the long vigil and wracked with anxiety. Deep down, a vague remorse was gnawing away inside her, brought on by her niece's wretched illness. Though she was the great-aunt's accomplice, she hadn't dared to tell her how she really felt now in her heart. Cowardice, a sense of shame, a grievous feeling of inferiority, all these things told her that she would have to see the tragedy through to the end. Yes, tragedy, because she already accepted that the curse was taking effect.

That very morning a medicine man came. But there was nothing at all he could do about the malady. Using *muzambo* (supernatural clairvoyance), he divined that a terrible spell had fallen upon the house and would very soon leave it empty. Nothing could stop it. And all for a sum of money found in the road and quietly withheld, despite all its owner's appeals.

'This is horrible, I'm dying when I'm still young and I haven't enjoyed one escudo of the money!' moaned Mussoko, her life entering its last twilight.

That night, amid a great thunderstorm, her two relatives were overcome by the poignancy of the occasion, as the great dam of their pent-up sorrow burst.

'Mussoko, Mussoko,' they wailed. 'What wrong have we done you, for you to abandon us so suddenly? Whatever are we to do without our niece?'

Their anguished cries brought the neighbours running in, full of concern.

'Isabel, Sule, what terrible thing has happened?' Donana asked them in surprise, but without the slightest suspicion of its cause.

'Donana, dear friend, we've no idea what brought this about! The poor thing has passed away after a mere week's illness!' They gestured towards the dead girl, who was stretched out on the bed, her face set hard in a grim expression of despair.

After another week, the whole neighbourhood was deeply perturbed yet again.

'Have you heard? Donana's died!'

'Died?!'

'It's true! Somebody, I don't know who, saw a red cockerel on her well!'

'A red cockerel?! That's the Evil One!...'

'Yes, it must be. It's something to do with that curse she called down... And when have we ever known rain in the season of the sea-haze?'

'She went to Ambriz, you know, because of that money of hers.'

'Oh, yes, she went there to call down the curse. She wanted the *jimbambi* to reveal who was the guilty one...'

'Serves her right! All she succeeded in doing was to bring down the curse on her own head... but just look at this rain!'

'The *jimbambi* are like that. They only come when there's rain or gales, they're not like other spells...'

'How frightful! The Evil One on her well! That's why there were all those crackling noises yesterday! It made me shudder, I can tell you!'

'Oh, when you hear a noise like that, it's the Evil One's mate beating her wings. Out in the bush, when they descend, if you get in their way and prevent them passing, they kill you! They may look like a cockerel and a hen but they run like partridges.'

'I know, I know. They even drop a few of their scales sometimes, which is what they have for feathers...'

'So just think, they saw the Evil One yesterday on the dead woman's well! I don't know whether it was the male or his mate...'

'Isn't it awful! But what use was it playing with spells like that? She only bewitched herself...'

'That's what comes of such meddling. If only she'd gone to church and prayed to Saint Anthony, the person who'd picked up the money would have shown up...'

'Yes, and she wouldn't have died...'

'Such is fate...'

Days later:

'Just think! Isabel's died!'

'How dreadful! One day her niece dies and then her! What terrible luck they're having!'

'When bad luck strikes a family, it doesn't let go.'

'But the strange thing is that those people who were present at the deaths of Mussoko and Donana have all been struck down by the same illness...'

'God forgive me, but I've even heard that it was Mussoko who picked up the missing money.'

'Really?'

'Well, I don't know, there are always rumours about, of course. We're all sinners, but they do say that she was the one who picked up the money. Poor thing, it appears that she wanted to hand it back to its rightful owner, but her aunt and great-aunt persuaded her not to.'

'God preserve us! And to think they're the older generation. Why on earth take other people's money?'

'And to think they were friends...'

'Some friends! Was their friendship really so superficial?'

'The old saying is right, isn't it? You can know people's faces but you don't know their hearts. What's such a pity is the poor girl's passing away at such an early age. I can still picture her, she was so attractive. And now her aunt...'

'God forgive me, her aunt's in the other world now, but what good was it, Mussoko being so good-natured, when her older relatives behaved the way they did? Thanks to the pigheadedness of her aunts, poor Mussoko and Donana have both passed away.'

'Donana had no idea how to call down a curse. What was the point of involving other people who had nothing to do with the money? Anyone who washes the corpse dies! Anyone present at the death dies! Even anyone who bewails the death, I ask you!'

'Well, she's died and she didn't get her money back. It just goes to show what can happen when people get in a rage! All that crying and shouting, and nothing at the end of it all! All that effort! But there you are. We'd probably all do the same!'

The deaths continued, one after another.

'Have you heard about the latest bit of bad luck? People are even dying in the street now!...'

'No! Who's the latest victim?'

'Don't you know? It's Catarina!...'

'Poor soul! Where?'

'In Cabino, near the railway line. The wretched woman was on her way to consult a medicine man about her health.'

'There it is, then! We're all done for, we're as good as dead.'

'You're quite right, cousin. We're all walking corpses. Our souls are already dead.'

And so, with constant high temperature, constant shooting pains, constant blood-spitting, the natives of that neighbourhood succumbed, one by one, without let-up, each and every one of them suffering increasingly from a harrowing black panic. As the curse had established, all those who attended the deaths of others paid with their lives for ignoring the grim warning. Fear-stricken, even friends began to abandon their customary solidarity and to avoid being present on such occasions. Even relatives, crushed by the same nightmare, were now beginning to desert their sacred vigil.

As if the catastrophe were not now enough, another horror overtook it: in an attempt to free themselves from the curse, members of Mussoko's family, now greatly reduced in numbers, were distributing the confounded money in the streets! This was terribly dangerous for children! However many warnings they might receive, how could they possibly resist such temptation? It would have been better not to divide it up. But they did so, a little here, a few escudos there, creating a diabolical challenge everywhere! Accursed money! Many innocent people had already perished because of it, and now, dear God, how many more?

'Don't ever pick up money in the street, d'you hear? It's bewitched! Just see how many people are dying!' the mothers warned their children.

But the harvest did not stop. With the fatal power of the spell, the vengeance was inexorably wrought. 'Anyone who washes the doomed one dies as well! Anyone who cuts his nails dies as well! Anyone who cuts his hair dies as well! Anyone who dresses him dies as well! Anyone who goes to be present at his death dies as well! Anyone who bewails his passing dies as well!' Where was salvation to be found? Faced with this great abyss, the medicine men were powerless, so terrible was the curse. Falling from the rain-clouds it implanted itself in the bodies of its unsuspecting victims, with its mystery it reduced them all to completing its baleful sentence: 'Die!'

'It's an epidemic!' announced the medical profession.

But the people weren't having that: supported by their medicine men, they retorted: 'What epidemic, indeed! It's the *jimbambi*!'

All those fatalities, with their two contradictory explanations, still weigh heavily on the souls of the inhabitants of Luanda; for them, the explanation was not a scientific one, it belonged to their spiritist dogma, just as in 1921, another very tragic year.

'The whites! What do they know?' some people asserted disdainfully.

Yet others adopted a similar superior attitude: 'But what d'you expect? Spells don't affect *them*...'

'It's like the Xamavo disaster in 1948, when the canopy of the Municipal Market collapsed...'

'That's right! The whites say the roof caved in because it was a very strong wind...'

'Strong wind! It caved in because of the *jimbambi...*'

'What do the whites know? Somebody lost her money there too, she went round asking everybody about it and then brought about disaster.'

'Why else should it only crash down on our people? The whites are all talk...'

'Quite so. What do they know? When a spell is cast on us blacks, then we die, we really do.'

'Yes, indeed! We're the descendants of Gola Kilwanji Kya Samba, our whole destiny is bad luck...'

> *With the rain, with the rain, with the rain it has rained,*
> *through the trap that they set,*
> *they all went off to the graveyard!*

So sing the people in a bitter song: the Song of the Xamavo Market.

THE POOR AND MEEK

A halcyon afternoon in March. A slightly cloudy atmosphere, a dying sun in its last gentle agony. A delightful breeze, wafting melancholy memories.

The Lisbon quayside is busily astir. Smart suits alongside shabby attire, everybody bustling about. Like sparks leaping from a fire, there is a crackling of emotion: mouths demanding, mouths kissing, eyes promising, eyes weeping; arms tremble in effusive handshakes, chests heave in warm embraces, souls are torn by the shedding of tears. Everyone senses the mood of wistfulness, born of affection.

The *Angola* sluggishly draws away from the quayside. There is a blast on the ship's siren. In a great sudden outburst, hundreds of handkerchieves wave in concert with the heartfelt cries of farewell.

Like fireflies on a dark night, questions light up the sad mist. Will they ever come back again? How many mothers will never see their sons again? How many wives their husbands? How much joy, how much bitterness will stem from this time of separation? Will they be happy in those fever-ridden places? Will they find the jobs, the fortunes, the enhancement of personal dignity that they so much desire? God help them in their aspirations.

Another blast on the siren. The widening gap weeps, just as love weeps, deep down in every soul. Frantically now, the handkerchieves flutter again, bidding their own farewell, as the last cries are swallowed up by the distance.

With one final hoot, the whole steamer vibrates as it heads into the gloom. Melancholy is intensified and surrounds everything like an icy fog. This last lament suggests the spasm of death.

Followed by the seagulls (the last messengers of those left behind), off they go in their floating world, exchanging Portugal for their distant lands. Will it be for ever? Nobody knows. Life is a question that oppresses the soul.

Sea and sky are now all that remain of the vortex of the passing days.

The ship was cutting across the swaying Atlantic, heading for the jaws of the horizon, on its hopeful way to Africa. Leaning on the rail, a passenger stares at the ocean. Magnetized by its grandeur, by its exciting and many-hued aspects, he takes refuge in mystical contemplation.

Like a page from the book of Nature, its troubled vastness was, in his eyes, an allegory of suffering. Whether in tenderness, or anguish, or anger, the voice of the ocean always carries a note of sorrow, always recalls a prayer to the Lord. Yes, it seems to implore forgiveness, an impetuous force living in a state of constant repentance. But God turns a deaf ear: no sooner does it humble itself, than it falls at once into fresh transgressions. It is for this reason that, wretched and angry, it never ceases to express its regret.

While he pondered these things, there suddenly occurred to the voyager a bright thought, as bright as rising moonlight: the analogy between the sea and man. In his imagination, both towed along a burden of torment, because they never mended their ways. In their explosive fury, they destroyed and killed and laid bare primitive emotions. To satisfy their overweaning ambition, they plundered and terrorized. Man and sea, how alike they were! Apparently good on the outside, yet perverse within! Do they experience love? If so, they sing. Are they sinful? If so, they writhe in sorrow. Are they unregenerate? If so, they pine and lament everlastingly.

'Ah, the sea! What a gripping lesson it has to teach us! It's one huge allegory!' exclaims the passenger, emerging from his daydream.

Eight o'clock in the evening. In the third class, in a cabin with ten berths, four men lie resting on their bunks. Like a pair of sunken eyes, two lamps glow feebly in the gloom. Through two port-holes there comes the mournful noise of the sea. Spasmodically, the ship creaks, its shudders intensifying the sombre mood. A torpor comes over them. Like a shadow cast by a cloud, a nostalgia enters their souls, transporting them back to their families.

Deep in thought, they resent the bitter taste of their leave-taking. Ah, the warm embrace of a mother now grew tighter, till it crushed one's heart! Poor woman! Advanced in years, imagining that she would never see her son again, she had sought to transmit all her warmth in that farewell kiss and to receive back, as a last memento perhaps, some hint of abiding affection. Sharp and painful, there impinged on the mind's eye of each man a recollection of his wife. Everything she'd had to say on that last day now resounded querulously and touched the chill depths. The echo of her voice was harrowing! It tore you open, ploughing the furrow of death! Smiling through his tears, each man sees a child: a bud opening amid four petals. The child is peacefully asleep in his cradle. Better not wake him or he'll start crying; just kiss the little angel while he slumbers. Alas! Will he cry later on, when he misses his father? And so, thoughts of their loved ones crackle upwards like sparks from the embers of love, forcibly reminding them that life is a grim business. As for destiny, what an extraordinary power it wields! Onward! is its motto, as it sends mortals hurtling headlong for good or ill. And what is life but a long chain of surprises?

From a nearby cabin could be heard a song, as someone accompanied it on a guitar:

On the strings of my guitar
I vent my yearning:
deep sorrow shall be mine
for the home I left behind.

My homeland, my homeland,
land of my heart,
on your hillsides high
stands the house for which I sigh.

Fate has called me away
to lands of mystery;
perhaps a humble grave
those lands for me will save.

'It sounds as though that guitar is as sad as its owner!' sighs one of the passengers, as the last chords die away.

'For us Portuguese, the guitar is our natural companion…' adds a second passenger.

'Of course it is, because the guitar accompanies so well any words that are sung from the heart. That poor fellow, for example, was making his guitar express every last drop of his homesickness.'

Silence falls. The rhythmic drone of the steamship, the sobbing of the sea went on peopling their dreams. At intervals, a chill breeze would waft into the cabin, bleak and piercing.

'Before coming aboard, I thought this would be just like being on a train...,' says a third voice, as its owner stirs, lighting a cigarette.

The first passenger suppresses the laugh that the simple remark had caused the others to break into, inquiring: 'Come on, man, didn't you notice that the ship travels on water?'

'So what? I've never seen a ship before.'

Poking fun, the second passenger has a go: 'Now look, João: two and two make four; seven and eleven make...; well, go on, how much?'

'What?!'

The second passenger repeats the question.

'Damn it! How Should I know? I'm no good at sums... I didn't go to school for very long...' confesses the simpleton, after a few moments' thought.

The first passenger, who had already toiled hard in Angola, mischievously turns to him again: 'Tell us one thing: have you ever been to Africa?'

'No, never, this is the first time I've ever left home.'

'In that case, you won't know the language the blacks speak,' the second passenger said.

'Of course I don't'

'Right then, listen,' advises the first passenger. 'One thing we've all got to learn is their language, especially the most common words. When they say to you, "*io mukua mulundu*", you should be pleased, because that's a compliment. They're saying that the white man is OK. And when you hear them say "*kuata o ngulu*", you should be very pleased with that as well, because it means that the white is a very clever man. I could teach you lots of other words, but there's no point. You'll learn it all soon enough anyway.'

The second passenger, who is equally knowledgeable about Angolan affairs, simply cannot contain himself any longer and bursts out laughing.

'You're pulling my leg, aren't you?' protests the poor yokel irritably.

'As if we'd do that, João,' replies his informant, suppressing a chuckle.

João takes umbrage, jumps down from his berth and leaves the cabin, muttering: 'It's not right at all! Not what you'd expect from well-brung-up people!'

The fourth passenger, who's been listening to the conversation in silence, cannot withhold his curiosity any longer: 'Come on, Silva, what does all that stuff really mean?'

'Well, *io mukua mulundu* means "this guy is a real peasant from the backwoods", whilst *kuata o ngulu* means "grab hold of this pig".'

Everybody collapses in mirth.

A quarter of an hour later, João reappears with a passenger from another cabin. Silently, João opens his suitcase and takes out a cheese, some bread and a bottle of wine. Sitting there on the case, they eat together amiably. In the absence of any glasses, João's guest suggests they drink straight out of the bottle. But João won't have that and claims it's all wrong that way. Off he goes to get a glass from the saloon.

'What an oaf this chap has turned out to be!' his guest comments cynically, trying to ingratiate himself with the other occupants of the cabin.

Instead of receiving any answer, a dumb silence is all he gets in return, as they discreetly watch him. Meanwhile, the glasses arrive. Appropriately enough, given the tropical heat, the drink is soon soaked up as they talk.

'Right then, João, any time you like, I'll be ready to offer the same to you,' the visitor says as he takes his leave, already up on his feet and rolling a cigarette.

'You off already?'

'Oh yes. Snack's over, time to move on.'

Joaõ laughs, a bit put out.

'Mustn't trouble you any further just now, João. It's good to be with you, but it's time I had a nap,' adds his companion, giving him a good pat on the back.

No sooner does he take his leave, than the first passenger inquires: 'Who's that character?'

'Oh, he's one of us but he works as a locksmith in Lourenço Marques.'[1]

'Have you known him a long time?'

'No, no, only here on board ship. We're both from the same area...'

Shortly afterwards, the first two passengers go out, whereupon João starts a conversation with the one remaining behind.

'Where are you making for?'

'Luanda.'

'Married?'

'No, no.'

'You're just like me, then.'

'If I don't get put off, perhaps I'll get myself a black woman out there. I'm told that those women, provided you direct them aright, are just the thing. I'm going to see whether I can manage to pile up some useful savings over the next few years. We're in 1930 at the moment; so, let's say, in about 1935 I should have enough to enable to give up. I'm a plumber by trade but I've been advised to set up in a cheap tavern.'

---

[1] Now Maputo, in Mozambique (TN).

'I'm a bricklayer, now you mention it; surely to God there's a good living to be made just by plying one's trade! Anyway, what d'you do with any children at the end of it all?'

'Children! Oh, somebody else could take them on... In any case, the mother would have to see to them...'

João didn't reply. He chose to show his disapproval for that way of thinking simply by keeping quiet. For him, the very idea was an outrage.

As he sat there in silence, he found himself going back through the little dramas of his own existence. When he was still a child, he'd lost his father and felt all the suffering that the loss had brought. His ailing mother had been in no position to let him enjoy growing up but had been forced to send him out to work at an early age, work which was too hard for his boyish strength. While others of his age were romping in the garden of boyhood, his miserable lot was to handle a bricklayer's tools, learning the trade with his godfather, who was long on drink and short on affection. Since João knew only too well what it was like to be without a father, he could never bring himself to show any enthusiasm for the cowardly conduct of men who abandon their own children. Such people were no better than dogs!

The plumber couldn't avoid noticing the effect of what he'd said and sought to defend himself by referring to his own background: 'Oh, come on! I got abandoned myself, you know!'

'All the more reason for not inflicting it on anyone else. A son without a father just trails about like an unstaked vine.'

'Hold on! It didn't kill me!'

'Yes, but, good grief, I had no father, either, because he died when I was little. I ate plenty of the Devil's bread as a result. Don't be so hasty, I say: to me this business of having children and then kicking them to one side like so many pups just isn't the decent thing to do, it's just not Christian. Still, each man has his own view of things...'

'What I say is this: seeing how my own father left me in the lurch, because I was born simply in answer to the usual need, then why shouldn't I do the same thing? It's too much bother otherwise.!'

'Yes, but damn it! People shouldn't trample on others just to improve their own quality of life... And anyway, what of the mother? Doesn't a woman earn less than a man?'

'Earn less? What's that got to do with it? Women don't need as much as men!'

'Now you're twisting things round. I'm talking about a woman who has no support, who has to live by the sweat of her own brow. If she has to struggle to earn her own daily bread, how's she going to cope with all those extra mouths? It's one thing for a woman's husband to die, it's quite another for him to go off and leave her with the burden of the children. Why, if she hadn't had a man, she wouldn't have any children, would she?'

'Well, obviously. Children don't just drop out of the sky like rain...'

'Well, there you are, then! If a man comes across a woman with nothing to fall back on, what right has he got to complicate her life for her? There's too much of that sort of lousy behaviour and too much suffering as a result.'

'Don't be so soft! You can't put the world to rights by that sort of talk... What does a ship's captain say when it's sinking? "Every man for himself!" Well, life's a ship as well. Don't you know the old saying "Sink or swim"?'

'Yes, but don't you know this one: "Don't do unto others what you wouldn't want them to do to you."'

'Ah, but turn it the other way round: "Do unto others what others have done unto you." Doesn't that amount to the same thing? Well?'

'Oh, let's leave it alone! Everybody's got his own way of looking at things...'

They fell silent.

The ship heroically moans its way onward, battling against the distance, zung... zung... zung...

It was eight o'clock in the morning when the *Angola* anchored off Luanda.[2] The bricklayer and the others go aboard a ship's boat. Moved by the vast African unknown, by that powerful sensation that people feel when faced with unforeseen surroundings, one old man let out a majestic utterance: 'Just look how beautiful it is! It's just like the bay of Rio de Janeiro!'

In the golden tropical sunlight the city wore a cheerful smile. Lazily and gracefully, it swept down in a vast picturesque amphitheatre that now looked quite different from the arid panorama it offered to those peering from the ship. The firm brush-strokes of the trees gave cool shade to the buildings.

As the bricklayer wandered idly through the streets, dodging the busy, blaring traffic, the general impression he received progressively blotted out the false notions he had entertained of what it looked like. The buildings stretched away in all directions and conveyed to him two particular characteristics: the old ones were staid, yet agreeable; the modern ones welcoming and fronted by gardens.

'None of this is a bit like we imagined it back home!' he exclaimed to those he was strolling along with.

'It isn't, is it? To tell you the truth,' added one of them, 'I thought the blacks still ate people...'

At one point, they crossed the square where the statue of Pedro Alexandrino stands.[3] Pedro Alexandrino was a former governor, mainly

---

[2] At that date there was not yet a landing-stage (AN).

[3] It was removed in 1976, after Angolan independence (TN).

of note for abolishing slavery in Angola. The bricklayer noticed a trickle of honey running out of the rear of the statue at a spot close to the anus.[4]

'That's rich! Just look,' he comments with a laugh, 'here the statues sh.. honey!'

The most impressive thing he noticed was the typical garb of the native women. This was characterized by lengths of cloth wrapped round their bodies, from their armpits to their heels, and a further piece of black cloth which served as a cape, covering the head and the back and falling across the bust as well.[5] So when the street traders with their baskets on their heads went by, proclaiming their wares in Portuguese, he gazed at them intently. As for the Kimbundu language, though he'd already heard such twaddle, as he called it, when they'd put in at São Tomé, well, that made him laugh as well.

'It's really true what they say,' he mused. 'Each land has its own customs, like each distaff has its own spindle.'

The bricklayer had been in Luanda for weeks. But the position he sought had not turned up: to save money, the builders had preferred to employ a native workforce. He began to lose heart. How was he going to cope, once his meagre savings ran out?

The heady feeling that he'd had at the outset of the adventure was now giving way to a sense of regret. The farm he'd dreamt of, the rise in social standing, his future well-being, all this was collapsing around him. Why'd he let himself be taken in by what he'd heard? If other people he'd heard of managed to pile up large sums, it was because they were destined to do so. Was he going to be in luck too? Not a bit of it! Why then had he followed in the wake of others simply because they'd been

---

[4] The statue is made of bronze and, for a period, because of a hole, it was populated by bees (AN).

[5] This form of dress is described at greater length in the novel *Uanga* (AN).

successful? It was a bad day when he'd made up his mind to leave for Africa!

In his distress he pictured himself back home. It was evening. The sun had declared a truce, and working people had sought peace from their daily toil. As usual, he was chatting to Teresa, his girlfriend, when the postman handed him a letter. Reading it had given him such pleasure, such an intoxicating feeling! Rocha, who lived out in Malanje, had written to tell him all sorts of wonderful things. 'Leave that life of yours back home,' the letter said, 'and come out here. It may not be all that it used to be, but it's still a marvellous country. If you don't succeed much in your own trade, then you can always set up a stall or a shop. A cheap tavern is a good idea, because the blacks don't stop until they've turned all their money into drink. So don't be daft, man. Give up what you're doing, because out here the cash is waiting for you.' Why not take his advice, then?

And so, that night, he'd tossed and turned restlessly, weighing up the past and calculating the future. After all, had he managed to store up any sort of nest-egg? No. He spent all he earned. Always round and round, without getting any further. So Africa it'd be, then. 'He who changes where he lives changes his luck,' went the old saying. To pay for the journey, he'd sell the little copse that used to belong to his mother. And when he got to that country where the money was, he'd save up all he could. And he'd let Teresa (his 'little Nanny Goat', as he called her) know about everything: what he earned, how much he saved and everything he was doing. And, after that, when he'd got a goodly sum saved up, to make up for the little copse, he'd buy a farm. But now, what a let-down! Now that he actually was in Africa, everything was the opposite of what he'd hoped. No savings, not even the security of a job! Africa was a temptation of the Devil! What rotten luck his was!

His head swam and, in the swirl of his disappointment, he remembered the critical example of another man he knew of who, doubtless lured out here in the same way, since he hadn't found any means of livelihood, had decided to do away with himself. But, before doing so, he'd wept, and what tears he must have shed, poor devil! In that last fiendish moment, or even earlier, as his reason gave in, perhaps he remembered, and why not? perhaps he remembered his family, mother, wife, children, there on the other side of the world, waiting for news of his promised good fortune. But everything had been an outright disaster. So... Oh Heavenly Father, forgive the man his weakness!

Shattered, discouraged, João drew strength from prayer: he was a Christian. Moreover, adversity had taught him to seek solace in his faith. When he prayed, he prayed for himself and then for others: God is the sweet refuge of love and suffering.

After many long weeks of despair, João manages to get a position as foreman at the Experimental Coffee Station out at Vila Salazar, known at that time as Dalatando.[6]

The plantation, in all its exuberance, was an introduction to the African forest. The tree crops (orange trees, lemon trees, cinnamon trees, camphor trees and so on) swept along in great long rows and, as if with the impulse of a universal brotherhood, here and there they intertwined their branches. Coffee, the main crop, with its bushes sprawling under the symmetrical protection of a variety of forest trees, stretched away endlessly. By day, cheerful birdsong gave a poetic touch to the surroundings. But, during the night, mixed with the baying of wild dogs, and the whining of the hyenas, the lugubrious clamour of so many other animals made it a sinister place. But nobody was surprised by such cries:

---

[6] As, once again, after independence (TN).

to all these animals, from the least offensive to the most ferocious, the forest was mother. Their collective voice was the voice of the forest itself. The only thing that terrified the natives was the call of certain birds, for theirs were cries of ill omen. Such bids only sang at the behest of a witchdoctor, never by chance; and, when their baleful call rang out, it was because the witchdoctor was casting, on request, a fateful spell.

Early each morning, after the bell rang out, walking at the head of a vast gang of workers, João would head out into the plantations, either to carry on with the work of the previous day or to set some new job in train. Grimly toiling, the workforce produced the delight that is coffee, which would later be sold, in tiny cups and to musical accompaniment, in some distant grand café. While they tended the crop, from time to time homesickness would spout forth like blood from a wound, immaterial yet like a lament rending the dense undergrowth.

João would stand and watch as they laboured. Everything amazed him: the flora, the fauna, even man's existence in this wild outdoor setting. He had already noticed that here the European led a plusher existence and no longer kept up his native modesty. As for the natives, they were communicative and frequently given to hearty laughter. He knew that the bulk of the workforce did not come from the same region: some came from Camabatela, others from the Dondo region, and others from localities the names of which he couldn't recall. Apart from having children, many of them had two, three or four wives. Just like him, others had sweethearts far away back home, though not as far away as his, longing for their return. There were two factors in living apart: one lay in the demands made by one's circumstances, the other was the extent of one's aspirations. The ideal that the latter constituted brought João great comfort, since the desire to improve his lot was a very different feeling for everyone to have. After all, blacks were no different from whites: they too had hopes and ambitions and likewise left their native villages in order to fulfil them.

João consoled himself with the thought of others making sacrifices in the pursuit of happiness and felt deep down a strange sensation that he couldn't put into words. Why, after all, shouldn't he succeed in the end? Others in the same situation had managed to make their dreams come true, hadn't they? He knew of plenty of cases where humble folk, with hard work and perseverance, had risen to enviable positions. He too, then, could win through, could get out of the morass in which he was vegetating: he trusted in God, he trusted in the future. His farm seemed to beckon to him, magically, from afar.

The forest, therefore, for all the sombre tales he'd heard about it, was so tempting – in spite of the Kifumbe, who lay in ambush to chop off people's heads to hollow out and sell as sugar basins; in spite of the powerful poisons that could penetrate through the sole of your boot and kill you almost instantly; in spite of the crocodiles that took you by surprise on the rivers and dragged you away into the shadows; and, among other terrors in popular belief, in spite of those wild animals that, through witchcraft, would attack anyone who someone else wished to have killed, the primeval forest was indeed tempting, was his great hope, and every month it gave him regular payments to add to his savings.

As what he yearned for gradually materialized, João had recovered his inner strength. Obsessively, he never grew tired of totting up his gains: every month he earned one thousand, two hundred *angolares*[7] and, of that amount, he easily saved some eight hundred or so: this meant that, after a year, he'd have nine thousand, six hundred *angolares* and in five years' time as many as forty-eight thousand *angolares*.

---

[7] The former *angolar* was the equivalent of the former Portuguese escudo (TN).

'Forty-eight thousand *angolares*! Oh! Little Nanny goat! Our farm!' he murmured, with his eyes gleaming, wide-open.

Sometimes he daydreamed while on duty. Whenever he came to, he noticed that some of the workforce were equally inactive, abstractedly puffing away at their pipes. Perhaps they were deep in thought, like he was, he mused. His curiosity would get the better of him, and he'd ask what they were thinking about. But in their simplicity – heh! heh! heh! – they took refuge in enigmatic little chuckles. What did a white man want to know about the life of a black man for? 'Mr João, he a good man, yes, but tell him what you feel in yo' heart, oh no!' But João persisted; he wanted to know what went on in the depths of a black man's soul.

'White man wanna know life of black man? We thinking of home, what happen when time over,' one of them told him one day, putting aside his usual shyness.

'Ah! Good, good! You'll need to work hard, then...'

'Oh yes, we working hard...'

Without developing his answer, the speaker looks at his companions, who were all busy weeding, and, after a pause, thrusts his hoe back into the soil. But, suddenly seized by an idea, he straightens up again: 'In Lisbon, who gen'ly do the diggin'?'

João smiles: 'The whites...'.

'Ah! So white men do work of black men?'

João smiles again: 'Oh yes, the white man does all the work there, in his own country...'

'Ah, yes...' the labourer says in surprise. 'And when he work, he sing too?'

'Yes, he does, especially at harvest time.'

'Not know what that is!'

Again João smiles: 'Harvest, that's what is grown and picked: beans, maize, potatoes...'

'Ah, yes. Thank you.' He glanced at his companions. Just as he began to hoe again, he adds cheerfully: 'So we sing now...'

At a signal, a chorus of voices rose up through the bright air, and the forest, with her mother's love, wept for her beloved children.

Eventually, a colleague advises João to get himself a woman to live with. After all, it would make life cheaper for him, and, that way, one bypassed unpleasant consequences. Not a virgin, though, the high bride-price made virgins a problem. Anyway, that wasn't the point: what mattered was to get a young girl. And there were some very attractive ones. If he liked, his colleague would deal with the matter: his own girl would choose one from among her friends.

'All right, then. He who leaps a lot risks falling a lot', agrees João.

Inquiries are made.

'Is he a good white man, d'you say?' remarks Conceição.

Back comes the answer from the other man's girl, with the help of a convincing smile: 'Of course he is! If he weren't, I wouldn't be talking to you about him... Accept, don't throw away a good opportunity.'

'All right, then.'

A few days later, João had a comely girl in his presence. Her appearance pleased him, it was just the bride-price that was a worry. Despite her not being 'first-hand', as they say in Africa, she asked for the following list of items: just for herself, three changes of clothes and two hundred and fifty *angolares*; for her family, two demijohns of wine, each one of five litres, and two bottles of port; and for a baby boy of hers, who needed to be weaned, a tin of condensed milk every two days and, every week, two packets of cornflour.

'Hell! And she's not even a virgin!' thought João. He turned in embarrassment to his friend, fixing him with a quizzical stare.

'Look, man, if it's a question of credit, I'll tide you over. Damn it, I'm not having you going without the girl for such a trivial reason!' He accompanied his remark with a wink then he turned to the girl, who was standing there, trying to read their facial expressions: 'Listen, Conceição: as it's Sunday today, sleep here tonight and then go and get your things tomorrow, all right?'

Next morning, feeling as though she owns the whole valley, she goes into the village to collect provisions. She walked on air. Birdsong, borne on the breeze, added to her contentment. Yes, indeed, a good white man! If only she could manage to live with him for a long time!

In her excitement, she even calls in at her own home to give her family the news: 'I've come for my things. Don't you want to come with me and see?'

Curiosity breaks out: 'What've you been given? Are we all going to get a drink? Go on, tell us.'

'Three changes of clothes... two five-litre demijohns... two bottles of port... and food for the baby...'

Like rockets at a party, the congratulations exploded joyously on all sides: 'Yeah! Congratulations! Many congratulations! God's on your side!'

Her female relatives and friends noisily gather round her, like flies round a honey-pot. But, to her disappointment, a salesman appears in the doorway, having been put up to this by João's rascally colleague, and now announces in a regretful tone that João can't meet what is required of him: he still owed lots of money to other people!

'Huh! So this white man is a scoundrel, after all!' sighs Conceição, feeling both shame and indignation at the same time. She utters a bilious grunt.

The members of her family are similarly outraged but show a hint of amusement as they join in her protest. 'Just like a foreman! Send him packing! Don't let him come back again, the penniless impostor!'

As a result of this incident, there was many an amused chuckle among the employees on the plantation. João's friend, ever helpful, once again fixes up another girl via his own girlfriend. Unlike the first one, this girl was not claiming any bride-price.

'If gentleman want me,' so went her conditions, ' he rob me from my family. I not want bride-price. I not chicken for sale...'

And so, under the careful watch of the stars, the forest was recovering from the embrace of Phoebus. The long grass whistled in the breeze, and the trees whispered gently.

Armed with stout sticks, two men from the plantation make their way along the road. One of them is nostalgically plucking a musical instrument called a *kambanza*. The other walks along in silence, deep in wily thoughts. Suddenly, he asks: 'Right, my lad, shall we have a go?'

The instrument falls silent, as if annoyed. 'Have a go at what?'

'Oh, come on! What d'you think? What we've come for...!'

'Eh? Are you drunk? I don't want to touch things that don't belong to me!'

'Don't be daft! D'you think she'd go and tell everybody about it? Are we doing this or not?'

The *kambanza* goes on calling up memories.

'Oh, my poor darling!' sighs the one playing it.

But his companion insists, wallowing in roguery by now. Yet his persuasiveness still meets with the same scorn.

Behind them, an arm of the river faded away with a sob.

'Let's wait here. There's the house,' warns the one who is carrying the now silent *kambanza*. Instead, he lets out a meaningful whistle.

A shadow looms up out of a background of shadows.

'Is it you two?'

'Yes, we came, like we said,' they reply.

'Let's go, then.'

And so, thanks to civilization, João was finally obliged to pay the bride-price, the stern formality of African marriage.

'João, are you up?' It is early one morning, and his colleague is nervously knocking at his door. 'Huh? What is it?'

'It's Júlio,' murmurs his girl, beside him.

The explanation is a hesitant one: 'Well, it's... I mean, could you possibly come round to my house...? I mean, right now, straight away?'

'What on earth for, I wonder?' muttered João, jumping up out of bed. 'All right, coming,' he called out. Hastily, he clambers into his trousers and slippers and rushes out of the bedroom.

'What's the trouble, Júlio?'

'It's my little lad, young Manuel, poor little chap! He's dying...'

João is shaken by the unexpected news. 'Oh no! Poor lad! How come?'

'That's just it! Having children is a wretched business! We bring them up, we make all sorts of sacrifices, and then, suddenly, wham! Along comes some upset and carts them off into the next world! But the thing is this: seeing how the little lad's never been baptized, right? And what with the priest only visiting the village from time to time, well, his mother's all in tears and says, well, you know, that the little fellow's not going to go to Heaven. So she wants you to baptize him.'

'But I've never done anything like that... I don't really know how to go about it,' stammers João.

As for Júlio, in spite of his being an atheist, he has to do this, not only to avoid further upset to the distraught mother, but also so as not to burden his own conscience. He explains what is wanted: 'Seeing as you're a Christian, just say the odd prayer or two... You put salt on his tongue, I think, like the priests do. Come on, please. It's the thought that matters.'

Off they went. From the night's struggle with advancing day, faint light, like a gentle sigh, came surging through the whole vast forest. Convinced that daylight would win through, the enthusiastic birds were already letting out their alleluias on all sides.

Someone started banging a length of old rail, as though it were a bell: it was the signal to wake up.

Striding silently along through the early dew, João was trying to understand his companion's attitude. How was it possible that an unbeliever like him could actually go against his own way of seeing things? Ah well, death works miracles in men's minds! After all, though they state the opposite, everybody, yes, everybody, deep down, really deep down in their souls, believes in God. Everything depends on the particular moment in time. And the truly great moment is the end of one's life. At that point, the big question really presents itself: 'Can there be a God?' And something replies: 'Yes, there's a God.' Why do people argue about it so much? Just human whims, that's all!

At Júlio's, a colonial oil-lamp lit the bedroom. Seated on the edge of the bed, his woman held a four-year-old child in her arms. Interspersed with feeble whimpers, he was having periodic convulsions. Sitting on a mat on the brick floor, two hastily summoned friends of hers were quietly trying to comfort her: 'Don't cry so! Let's wait and see what God does. Perhaps he'll get better.'

Clutching a burning candle, João came close to the dying boy and uttered the following words with all due solemnity: 'Manuel, I baptize thee, in the name of the Father, and of the Son, and of the Holy Spirit, amen!' so saying, he pushes a pinch of salt into the little closed mouth. 'Go in peace, go unto the Lord!'

Following his entreaty and example came a chorus of prayers: 'Our Father... who art in Heaven...'

An anguished silence enveloped the struggling child. Profanely, up in the blueness of the sky, there sang out the cries of the birds. The little boy's eyes were dull, half-closed and were filled with a sad poignancy; it was as though they already beheld Heaven. Finally, a sob rises up from the quietness in which he lay.

'Now he's with the angels!' whispers João.

His heathen father, quite overcome by it all, felt changed somehow, felt very tiny within himself: the reason is that God, just as many years before, in those distant days of sweet illusions, occupied once more the altar of his soul.

Outside, loud and long, the makeshift bell was now calling people to work. But at that moment it seemed to represent a death-knell.

'No, no, no! My son, my son! Why've you left me? What crime have I committed for my son to die?' lamented the mother in a singsong voice.

Borne along by his deep urge to succeed, João continued to pile up his hoard as each month went by. In no way did he feel overshadowed by those who did well in the cities: yes, many of those who made a splash there with their money had once been just as wretched as he had been. But he felt no envy towards them. One day he'd be their equal.

Yes, why envy them? Didn't gigantic buildings rise up out of the ground, stone by stone? Grain by grain, didn't a hen fill its craw? So he'd win through. Just like those who'd gone through poverty before him, he too would have a car, he too would frequent the grand cafés, he too would enjoy life in all its splendour. But he would always do the right thing. Never would he take advantage of people who were down on their luck, never! No, he wasn't going to wallow in his money: anyone who tramples on sick people for his own ends simply digs a hole for his own future torment! Ah yes! If one day he got rich, really rich, he'd found a home for waifs and strays, for orphans, for all those children who hadn't got a roof over their heads! With the contribution of the sweat of his brow, he'd like to work towards the extinction of the bonfire of human misery. After all, his own past was still painful to remember!

In its turn, the great lonely forest intermittently joined in with the songs of the everlasting poor and meek.